PAYBACK

This book is dedicated to the brave young woman
who told me her story

First published in Great Britain and in the USA in 2009 by
Frances Lincoln Children's Books, 4 Torriano Mews,
Torriano Avenue, London NW5 2RZ
www.franceslincoln.com

First paperback edition 2009

British Library Cataloguing in Publication Data available on request

ISBN: 978-184507- 935-2

Set in ITC New Baskerville LT

Printed in the UK by CPI Bookmarque, Croydon, CR0 4TD

1 3 5 7 9 8 6 4 2

PAYBACK

ROSEMARY HAYES

FRANCES LINCOLN
CHILDREN'S BOOKS

CHAPTER ONE

Halima

I was only four years old when my father came back. I remember standing beside my mother – my *ammi* – outside our house in the village in Pakistan, staring towards the distant mountains, waiting for him.

Ammi knelt down beside me up and kissed my neck. 'Look at those grand mountains, Halima,' she whispered. 'How small they make us feel!' She was young and pretty then, my *ammi*. I snuggled against her and breathed in her smells – the familiar smells of cooking and the oil she put in her hair.

We didn't see much of my father when I was little. He was important in the village because he owned land, but mostly he was away working in England, earning money to send back to the family.

I was only two years old when he went away. My mother and the other women had been preparing for his homecoming for days, cooking up a feast, laughing and shouting together, cleaning the house and then putting my brothers and my sister and me in clean clothes to greet him.

I couldn't stand still any longer. I broke away from Ammi and ran to and fro, excited and noisy, getting in everyone's way. Ammi caught up with me and picked me up, laughing.

'Look at your clean clothes – dusty already,' she scolded. But she wasn't really cross.

We watched as the minibus laboured up towards the village from the plain beneath. The excitement mounted. There were shouts as it came nearer, then people started waving and my brothers and my cousins jumped up and down.

'He's coming! He's nearly here!'

I don't know what I expected – perhaps a tall, handsome man in flowing robes. I joined in the excitement, clapping my chubby hands, wriggling in Ammi's arms.

Then, at last, the dust-covered minibus shuddered to a halt and I saw him climb down from it. A stout, short man with balding dark hair. He wasn't the handsome hero I had imagined. I remember feeling disappointed as he came towards us, all smiles, his arms full of presents, everyone crowding round him, talking, greeting him, touching him.

But not me. I was shy and awkward with him. He took me from Ammi's arms and I squirmed and tried to get away when he lifted me up to hug me.

'Come on, little Halima, give your baba a kiss,' he said, and his smile turned to a frown as I twisted my face away from his.

I went rigid in his arms. He gave a grunt and put me down, and I ran back to Ammi and clutched her legs.

My mother stroked my hair and smiled nervously. 'Be patient,' she said to him. 'She'll get used to you again. You'll see. She'll soon get to know her baba again.' But my father moved away, irritated, as I sucked my thumb and peeped out at him from behind Ammi, my eyes wide.

He was a distant figure in those early days; none of us really knew him. It was Ammi who cared for us – for Khalil and Imran, my two brothers and for Asma, my sister, and me. Ammi accepted my father's long absences without question. She had married my father when she was only thirteen and she never questioned his authority.

Mostly, those early years in the village were happy times for us – though even then, they were happiest when my father was away. I was the youngest of the four children, trailing along behind the others. Imran was my favourite of the two boys. He was always teasing me, always laughing, and as I grew older I attached myself to him whenever he let me.

'Race you to the water!' he would say.

He knew I couldn't race him, but he'd pretend I was overtaking him as I panted behind, until we reached the irrigation channels which led to the fields.

'Let's cool you down, little sister,' he'd shout, wallowing in the channel and then standing up with rivulets of water running down his lean brown chest, his hair plastered to his head, splashing me until I was weak from giggling and squealed for him to stop.

Imran was bright as quicksilver, never still, always on to the next thing.

'Tea!' he'd call out, and we'd race through the village, dodging women coming back from the well with heavy water jars on their heads, and make our way to the tea-shop. I would lurk at the edge of the crowd as Imran proffered his five rupees for a cup of sweet, milky tea.

'Where did you get the money from?' I always asked him this as we shared the drink, but he never told me, just tapped the side of his nose and grinned.

The owner of the tea shop had a television and it was on all the time, so Imran and I would sneak a look at programmes we'd never be allowed to watch at home, hoping none of our relations would see us and tell Ammi.

Sometimes we'd run down through the orchards to the fields. The tracks were always bustling with grubby barefoot children, carts towed by buffaloes, battered tractors and herds of goats. Once, when we stopped at Baba's land and watched the men working with their hoes and scythes, I asked Imran why Baba was away all the time.

Imran shrugged, and snatched at a dry stalk of grass. 'He makes more money over in England,' he said. Then he added, 'But he says one day we'll all go over there to live with him.'

I remember that moment. Some women were toiling along the side of the track, bent double under huge bundles of twigs. They didn't look up as they passed us, but I was conscious of their presence as I stared back at Imran and I felt my heart beat faster. Surely he'd got it wrong?

I frowned. 'You and Khalil,' I said. 'He'll take you and Khalil to England, but not us. Surely not Ammi and Asma and me.'

Imran was on the move again, running along the track. 'Who knows?' he shouted back over his shoulder.

For a while I stayed where I was, looking into the distance, out over the Peshawar plain and the Kabul river which snaked through it, gleaming like dull silver in the harsh sunlight.

☪☪☪

So much has happened since then. We left the village long ago, but I still think of it and the smallest thing can trigger my memory and bring the place sharply into focus. A hot steamy day or the crackling of a fire and I'm there again, smelling the buffaloes, the wood smoke from fires, the warm fruit, the sticky sweetness of sugar cane and the petrol fumes from the decorated minibus that drove to and from the bazaar in the town nearby.

And the kite flying and the magnificent mountains – always the vast, distant, mysterious mountains which made me feel so tiny and insignificant.

The sounds of village life are still with me, too. The chattering children, the creaking carts carrying sugarcane to the factory, women talking and laughing as they went about their chores in their loose tops and trousers, with scarves over their hair.

Memories of laughter and gossip and dust and steamy dampness – and of being part of a huge extended family with a secure routine to my life.

I cling to the memories, trying to make sure I don't lose them. For I can never go back to my village. I am an outcast and I would not be welcome.

CHAPTER TWO

It was all my father's doing. He made the deal when I was eight years old. Of course, I knew nothing of it then. I knew nothing of it for years afterwards.

He was back in the village again. We hadn't seen him for two years and I was still awkward with him and found it hard to accept the authority of this stranger in the middle of our family. Khalil, the oldest, was scared of him, but Imran was confident and had an easy charm. He was Baba's favourite. Even as an eight-year-old, I could see the way Baba's eyes softened when he looked at Imran and how he smiled at him, proud of his quick wit and ready humour.

'You'll see,' he said to Ammi and the mass of uncles and aunties and cousins who were listening. 'You'll see. He's a clever boy. My Imran will make something of himself.'

And Imran grinned and ran off, while Khalil stood around looking spare. Khalil longed for my father's approval, but he didn't have Imran's winning ways.

☪☪☪

That time when Baba came back, there was some crisis in the village. Something to do with his land, and he was very worried about it. Ammi told us to keep out of his way and not bother him. We didn't need telling twice, for whenever anyone spoke to him he was short-tempered and grumpy. Even Imran couldn't please him.

'Go away, boy,' he shouted. 'Get out of my sight.'

And then, suddenly, Baba was all smiles again, patting the boys on the head, hugging us girls. Apparently some guy – some distant relation – had solved the problem, and the problem, whatever it was, was fixed.

One day not long after this, I was with my cousins on our way back from school. I remember that it had rained a lot that week and I'd missed some lessons. There wasn't enough space for us all inside the school, so some classes were taught in the courtyard and if it rained, the children in the courtyard were sent home.

But that day it was fine and sunny and my lessons hadn't been interrupted. As I walked back towards our house, I saw my father standing by one of the wells with another man. I didn't know it then, but the other man was the relation who had solved the problem with the land. My dad was laughing and talking to him and I saw them shaking hands, and then my dad put his arm around the man's shoulders.

Baba saw me and beckoned me over. He was all smiles. 'Come here, little one,' he said. 'I want you to meet my cousin and my very good friend.'

Nearly everyone in the village was related. We were all members of the Pushtoon tribe and we were all cousins of some sort. But I'd never seen this cousin before.

The man bent down, smiling, and cupped my face in his hand. He looked up at Baba.

'Youngest, eh?'

Baba nodded. 'She's a good, obedient child,' he said.

I was surprised. Baba never praised his daughters. I blushed and looked down at my dusty feet.

The man straightened up. 'Good and obedient, you say? Excellent, excellent.'

Then Baba gave me a little push. 'Off you go, Halima. Go back to Ammi. She's waiting for you in the house.'

And so I trotted off home. Our house was one of the biggest in the village and one of the oldest. It had two storeys and was made of brick, and the first floor was completely surrounded by a wall so that outsiders couldn't peep at the women in the back yard.

Ammi was at the door to greet me. She'd been watching for me and she'd seen Baba call me over and show me to his new good friend. She said nothing. She just put her arms round me and I remember that she stayed there, holding me tight, looking over my head, back towards my father, until I wriggled free.

The incident meant nothing to me and I soon forgot it. It was only later – years later – that it all came back to me and I realised what it meant.

On that visit, Baba was only with us a few weeks before he went back to his job in London. Before he left, he called us all together.

'Good news,' he said, smiling at the two boys. 'Khalil and Imran, you are to come back to London with me.'

Imran leapt up and did a dance round the room. He punched Khalil on the arm.

'London, brother. We're going to London. See, I told you Baba would take us there!'

The boys were excited, particularly Imran, but London meant nothing to me then. It was a strange, faraway place, a place where Baba worked and where he made money to send back to us, a place I'd seen on television. Ammi didn't let us watch much television but we were allowed to watch the six o'clock English news. At home we spoke Pushtu and we understood Urdu and a little English, and although Ammi spoke no English, she wanted her children to learn it. Some of our neighbours had Sky television and we longed to watch it, but Ammi despised them and it. 'Showing off,' she would mutter.

I remembered what Imran had told me when we were walking in the fields – but I thought he must have got it wrong. Baba had said that the boys should go back to England with him but there was no mention of us girls – or Ammi – going with him, even though Asma was older than Imran. Like me, she would stay and help Ammi at home in the village.

Baba went on. 'Khalil and Imran will go to school in England and live with me and their uncles.' And, as he spoke, his eyes rested on Imran. 'They will have a good education in England. Maybe they will go to university there.'

But his next remark surprised us all. Baba smiled broadly and flung out his arms.

'Then, when I come back in two years' time,' he went on, 'the rest of you will come back to England with me. We shall all be together again.'

Ammi's eyes flew open in surprise. It was obvious he'd said nothing to her about this. But then, Pushtoon men can do what they like within their families and Ammi never questioned any decision Baba made. She said nothing, just looked down at her hands. Any questions or doubts were quickly squashed.

Allah willed it. She went wherever her husband led.

Asma and I were sitting on either side of Ammi and she drew us closer to her and tightened her hold on us.

Back then, I thought that my *ammi* would always be there to comfort and protect me.

How wrong I was.

☪☪☪

Not long after this, all our cousins and aunties and uncles gathered together to say goodbye to Baba and the boys. It took ages, because everyone got a hug and people pressed presents into Baba's hands and wished them all well. Then at last, the minibus lumbered into the village and stopped beside the crowd of people, the engine still throbbing. Baba, Khalil and Imran heaved their backpacks, cases and rolled-up mats into the minibus and then hung out of the windows, shouting and waving.

Ammi, Asma and I stood and waved them off. We watched as the minibus wove its way across the plains between the fields towards Mardan, the nearest town. Then it turned a corner and was lost to sight.

I imagined the bus jolting its way along the road to Mardan. It was a journey I knew well. I often went to the bazaar there with Ammi. It was big and bustling and noisy and when we went, I stayed close to Ammi while she searched for goods we couldn't buy in the village. Many of the local women did beautiful embroidery and I would squat down by their mats spread out on the ground and stare at it, wondering at its intricacy.

Mardan was the furthest I had ever been, the extent of my world. I thought that I was going on to secondary school in Mardan, but now Baba was saying that we were all going to England and to schools in London next time he returned.

After Baba and the boys left, life resumed its seasonal rhythms. The hot humid summer, the monsoon season when everything seemed damp, the cooler winter days, the sowing and harvesting of crops, the fetching of water, the milking of buffaloes, cooking and sewing.

I loved sewing.

'You have a good, steady hand, Halima,' said Ammi one day, as I was bent over a piece of embroidery.

I looked up at her and frowned. 'I'll never be as good as you.'

Ammi sat down beside me. 'I couldn't do this when I was your age,' she said. 'You will make beautiful things when you are older, you'll see.'

I was pleased to hear this and after that, whenever she could spare the time, she would sit down and show me how to do more complicated stitches and create patterns.

My days were full. I went to the primary school in the mornings for lessons and to the mosque school in the afternoons to learn the Koran. And whenever I could snatch a moment, I would embroider.

I had to help with the housework, too, and Ammi often sent me to buy things from the small shops in the village. Sometimes pedlars came to our house to sell household goods we couldn't get in the village. They sold shiny trinkets and jewellery, too, and I loved fingering these and holding them up to the light so that they winked and sparkled.

I didn't think about my future. Baba said we were going to live in England and, like Ammi, I accepted it without question. I didn't know what this meant, but I knew the family would be together and that there were lots of other uncles and aunties and cousins already living there. If I thought about it at all, I probably imagined London as a bigger version of Mardan.

So the two years went by, the pattern of life hardly changing. Occasionally there was trouble in the village and the culprit was punished by the elders. The punishments were brutal and this certainly brought home to us children the power of the elders. So we did our best to avoid them.

Girls, particularly, were expected to be quiet and modest and not cause our families any anxiety, so Asma and I kept a low profile.

As the time for departure grew closer, I began to question Ammi.

'Will we come back?'

'Yes Halima, of course we'll come back. We'll come back to visit, for sure. We'll come back for family weddings.'

'Will we still have our house – and the buffaloes?'

Poor Ammi. She was probably as ignorant as I, but she did her best.

'Everything will be the same,' she said. 'Nothing will change.'

Nothing will change. It became a sort of mantra.

'Do you want to go?' I asked my sister

Asma laughed. 'Of course, silly! It will be an adventure. London is a big city, there will be lots to do, lots to see.'

'What will our school be like? Will it be like the one in Mardan?'

She shrugged. 'It will be better. Undoubtedly it will be better.'

But I knew she was nervous.

And so was Ammi. She busied herself sorting out what we needed to take with us. Several people in the village knew London. Some of the men had worked there for a while and their families went back and forth, so Ammi was given plenty of advice from all the uncles and aunties. There was a telephone connection to the village, so she heard from Baba, too.

'Bring plenty of warm clothes,' he shouted down the line.

'Hush,' said Ammi, laughing, 'Your voice is so loud, you will turn the buffaloes' milk sour!'

And then one day, in the early summer heat, Baba came to fetch us. He brought the boys back with him.

Suddenly it was really happening. We were going to leave everyone and everything.

The last few days passed in a whirl of activity. It was too quick for me. I needed time to say goodbye to my playmates, to the aunties, to the buffaloes, but Ammi kept me busy running errands for her, helping to check lists, going off to buy last minute stocks of this and that.

The morning of the day we were due to leave, Baba announced that he needed to look at his land, to check everything one last time.

On impulse I said, 'May I come with you, Baba?'

I don't know what made me say it, because I was sure he would say no, but he looked at me for a long time, frowning, before he replied, 'Hurry then, Halima, we shall have to be back before the bus comes.'

We walked out of the house one last time and down through the orchards to the fields. Baba stopped and breathed deeply. He stared critically at his neatly planted crops and then for a long time he gazed up at the mountains, clear and sharp against the hot blue haze.

Then he said an extraordinary thing. He turned and looked me full in the face and, for the first time in my life, I sensed some uncertainty in his voice.

'You will guard my land when you come back, won't you, Halima?'

I was puzzled. Why me? I was only ten, and a girl. Surely, when we came back, the boys would oversee the land for him. Then Baba gave a short laugh.

'But all that is in the future, eh?' he said. 'Now we must concentrate on making the best of our time in England.' And he turned on his heel.

'Yes Baba,' I said, trotting behind him to keep up, as he strode back into the village, taking no account of my short legs. He didn't look back and he didn't wait for me to catch up. When, at last, we had retraced our steps I was breathless and hot, with a bad stitch in my side.

And there I stood panting, the sweat trickling down my back, surrounded by a crowd of well-wishers, waiting for the trusty minibus to take us to Mardan on the first leg of our journey to London.

CHAPTER THREE

The boys – and my father – were insufferable on the plane journey. Imran and Khalil knew it all. They had been in England for two years and they knew all about air travel. My sister, Asma, had been bursting with confidence when we set off, but I could see it was ebbing away.

She nudged me as we took our seats. 'See those women over there,' she whispered. I glanced along the row. There were several Western girls, their heads uncovered, shrugging their backpacks off their shoulders to stow in the overhead lockers. We'd often seen women like this in Mardan, loud and confident, laughing together with Western men, so unlike Ammi or the other women from our village. But we'd never been quite so close to them. I turned to Imran who was still standing in the aisle, waiting to sit down. 'Are all the women like that in London?' I whispered.

He laughed. 'You're such a baby, Halima. You don't know a thing.'

I frowned, not daring to ask more. And if I was

already getting nervous about our new life, poor Ammi was terrified. I was in the middle seat and she was next to me, squeezed up against the window, kneading her hands in her lap, her eyes large as she stared around her. When at last we took off, she closed her eyes and I could see her lips moving in prayer.

My father and brothers all sat together in the seats in front of us, noisy and laughing. I whispered to Asma, 'Baba should look after Ammi. She's so scared.'

Asma was in the aisle seat. She looked across at Ammi and sighed.

'Baba will never comfort her,' she said quietly. 'We are the ones who must do that, Halima.'

I frowned, and looked at Asma more closely. In the last year she had blossomed. She was fourteen and of marriageable age – a woman now. Looking back, I think that, even then, she saw Baba for what he was.

'Will Baba find you a husband in London?' I asked.

Asma smiled. 'Perhaps.'

'But you said he wants you to finish your education there,' I said, puzzled.

'Yes. Can you believe that?'

I knew what she meant. It was almost unbelievable. On the one hand Baba treated us girls with such disdain, and on the other he wanted us to have a good education. I would never understand him.

'I suppose he'll look for a husband when I'm through school,' she said.

I snuggled nearer her, suddenly very glad of her presence.

'Will it be very different over there?'

Asma nodded. 'Of course it will be very different, you silly girl. You've seen all the photos Baba brought back, you've seen pictures on the television. You know what it's going to be like. Khalil and Imran are always going on about it.'

'Huh!' I said. I was fed up with hearing about London from my two brothers. They kept bragging about their new experiences, their schools and their new friends. They spoke good English now and sometimes they spoke to each other in English – really fast, so that Asma and I couldn't understand them. They had become so arrogant. I didn't want to take their word for anything. I wanted to see for myself, experience everything for myself, make my own observations. Nothing they said to me really sank in because I wasn't there. I tried to imagine how our house would look, how we would live, what the neighbours would be like, and my new school.

But I gave up. It was too hard. Pictures on the television, photos and descriptions from the boys were not enough. I couldn't make that leap of imagination.

I moved away from Asma and turned to Ammi. I took her hand in mine. 'It will be good, Ammi. You'll see.'

She said nothing, just squeezed my hand and then turned back towards the window, but not before I saw the tears in her eyes.

Poor Ammi. How she would miss her friends and relatives in the village, and how she would yearn for those reassuring, ever-present mountains. Would she ever be able to learn a new language and a new way of life?

Once we had been in the air for a while, I started to enjoy the flight. I kept sneaking looks at the other passengers and wondering about their lives. Most of them were Pakistani. Were they all going to live in England or were they just visiting? And what of the Westerners? How long had they been in my country? Were they business people or tourists? What had they been doing there?

Being served with our own little trays of food was fun, and even going to the toilet was an adventure. Once I discovered where it was, I trotted back and forth several times. I'd never seen a flushing toilet before and the first time I pressed the knob, as instructed by Imran, the loud *whoosh* took me by surprise and I leapt back in fright and hit my back against the door.

The hours went by and the novelty began to wear off. We grew bored and restless. Asma and I both dozed a little but I don't think Ammi did. She spent most of the journey sitting upright in her seat, staring ahead.

Then at last the aeroplane started to make its descent. Ammi closed her eyes again and put her hands over her ears.

'They hurt,' she muttered.

Khalil screwed round from the seat in front. 'If your ears hurt, Ammi, keep swallowing,' he said.

How irritating he is, I thought. But he was right. It did help.

As we flew lower and lower, I leaned over Ammi trying to see out of the window, but it was gloomy and cloudy and it wasn't until we were much lower that I could make out the buildings and lights and roadways beneath us. And as the plane touched down and we lurched eventually to a standstill, Ammi finally opened her eyes and let out a huge sigh.

'Allah be praised,' she whispered, and smiled at me.

Baba was irritable as he shuffled us all through Passport Control and he seemed diminished when he spoke to the officer at the desk. I'd never seen him like this, obsequious and oily. I watched him closely as he pretended to understand what was being said. He smiled and nodded constantly, wringing his hands.

Eventually, Imran stepped forward and answered the questions for him, translating them back into Pushtu. Baba continued to smile until we had passed through Immigration and then he scowled at the humiliation of it all and strode ahead, leaving us to scuttle in his wake.

It was then I realised that he spoke very little English. All these years in England, and he hardly spoke the language!

Was he always like this? Was he only overbearing on his own home ground? This was a Baba I didn't recognise.

We stuck close together in the arrivals hall. Only the boys seemed confident. Baba blustered and sweated and looked more and more uneasy. The boys hauled our cases off the carousel and on to trolleys and at last we made it through Customs.

Then, as we came out, there were even more people. It seemed that half of Pakistan was there to greet their relatives. We were jostled and elbowed as we stared helplessly about, looking for the uncles and aunties who were supposed to meet us.

'Where are they, Baba?' I asked.

Baba was wiping his face with his sleeve.'Be quiet, girl!' he snapped.

'There! There they are,' shouted Khalil, pointing.

And then, for the first time, Ammi smiled. A

big, wide smile as she waved and started running towards them.

I was swept up in the rush and unknown arms were hugging me. 'So this is little Halima! And Asma – how pretty she is! How grown-up. We'll soon be finding a husband for her!'

I looked up at the sea of faces surrounding me, all speaking Pushtu. We could have been back in Pakistan.

Eventually, we disentangled ourselves and rolled our trolleys out of the building and over to the multi-storey carpark. I tucked a stray curl of hair beneath my headscarf and looked up towards the leaden sky.

Although there had been a big crowd of relatives to greet us when we arrived, somehow we all fitted into three cars. Imran got into the front seat with one of the uncles and I squeezed in behind with Ammi and Asma. 'See, girls,' said Imran, turning round to grin at us. 'Every uncle has a car of his own.'

We nodded, suitably impressed.

'And now,' he continued. 'I'll show you our house.'

CHAPTER FOUR

Another journey! And still squeezed in beside Ammi. I was very confused about all the uncles and aunties, but whichever uncle it was drove confidently, stopping and starting, weaving in and out. I'd never seen so many cars and buses and lorries, even in Mardan.

When we had been driving for nearly an hour, mostly in heavy traffic, I said to Imran, 'Are we still in London?'

The uncle heard me and laughed. 'It is a huge city, Halima, and the airport is right the other side from where you are going to live, in Walthamstow.'

Walthamstow. I tried to pronounce the word but I couldn't get my lips round it.

The uncle laughed again. He was a fat, jolly man. 'Good try, Halima. We'll be there soon.'

I settled back in the seat and continued to stare out of the window. Although it was summer time, there was no sun. No blue sky. No mountains. Just streets and houses and shops.

'Ah!' Ammi pointed to a mosque, sitting between

two other buildings. 'Is this our mosque, uncle?'

The uncle nodded. 'It is the one we go to.'

Then, suddenly, Imran called out, 'The next street, Ammi. The next street is where we live.'

We all craned forward and the car slowed down to turn. I noticed shops nearby, all sorts of shops, many of them selling the sort of goods we had at home in Pakistan. I also noticed women in headscarves, women who looked no different from Ammi.

Ammi was beginning to relax. Here were things she understood. Her face brightened.

'There's a market here twice a week,' said Imran. 'Fruit and meat and vegetables.'

'But will they understand us?' asked Ammi.

'Yeah. There are lots of Pushtu and Urdu speakers round here. And anyway, you'll soon learn English.'

'But Baba doesn't speak much English, does he?' I asked.

Imran frowned. 'Enough,' he said shortly.

Then the car stopped outside a narrow house with a door which opened out on to the street. Ammi, Asma and I stared up at it.

Baba had bought the house for us just before he left for Pakistan. Before that, he and the boys had been living with one of the uncles.

'We shall be together at last,' sighed Ammi.

A horn honked and one of the other cars drew

up behind us, then the third behind that. Eveyone spilled out on to the pavement and began talking and gesticulating and getting out the luggage.

Baba unlocked the front door and ushered us in. Excitedly, Ammi, Asma and I ran in and out of the rooms and up and down the stairs.

'Girls, this is your room,' said Baba, opening a door off the upstairs landing.

Asma looked disappointed. 'Do we have to share, Baba?'

Baba frowned. 'Ungrateful girl,' he said. 'All these years I have been living with the uncles to save money, and now you complain when I have bought you a house.'

'Sorry, Baba.'

I looked at Asma. She was blushing. She hated it when Baba was angry. She would do anything to keep the peace. And I felt for her even more when we saw that Imran and Khalil had a bedroom each.

'The boys need quiet to study,' said Baba.

And we girls don't? I thought.

The kitchen was smaller than I'd imagined but it was already well stocked and the aunties had been busy cooking food for our arrival.

Ammi clapped her hands together. 'Oh, those smells,' she said. 'They remind me of home.'

Baba scowled at her. 'This is your home now.'

'Of course,' said Ammi quietly.

We all realised how hungry we were when we sat down to pumpkin soup followed by *pokara.* Everyone was talking at once. Ammi was animated again, relieved to be amongst her own. There were offers of help from all sides.

'I'll take you to the market and show you the shops,' said one auntie.

'And tomorrow, girls, I'll show you where your schools are,' said another. 'Halima can walk to her primary school. It is just at the end of the road. And Asma will take the bus.'

Baba cleared his throat. 'Asma, some of your cousins are already pupils at the school. It is for girls only.'

'A very good school,' chipped in another auntie. 'And you don't have to pay.'

Asma nodded and smiled.

Baba leant back in his chair. Now that he had eaten, his temper had improved.

'Yes,' he said, belching. 'All my children will have an excellent education, God willing.'

'How lucky they are,' said Ammi.

There was no trace of irony in her voice but I couldn't help thinking how little education she herself had had. She was already married and helping to run a house at thirteen, and pregnant with Khalil at fourteen.

CHAPTER FIVE

And so our life in England began.

There were a few more weeks to go before the start of the new school year and during that time we got to know the London cousins. We visited relations and the aunties took Ammi, Asma and me around the shops and to the mosque. And most weekends, the aunties and uncles showed us different parts of London. Once they took us to the West End, and we rode on an open-top bus.

Ammi was so excited. 'Look, children!' she said, pointing to Big Ben and the Houses of Parliament. 'Look! We saw those places on television back in the village!'

Sometimes we went to the cinema with some of the aunties, but we were only allowed to see the films of which Baba approved; I loved the warmth and darkness of the cinema and the magic of the stories they showed.

And several times we all went out to eat, crowding into a big local restaurant where nearly all the people were Pakistani like us, and the food a version of what we had been used to back in the village.

In some ways, life was completely different. The everyday smells were different, the skies were greyer and there were no fields, orchards, ancient tractors or buffaloes – and certainly no mountains! But inside the house, Ammi created a mini Pakistan. Smells, ornaments, fabrics – they were all familiar friends.

Ammi was worried that she'd never make herself understood when she went shopping. At first, Asma and I always went with her if the aunties weren't around. But soon she became more confident.

'The people in the shops all speak our language,' she said, beaming.

Asma laughed. 'That's because you only go to the shops the aunties show you, Ammi.'

We saw our relations most of the time and only went to the shops where they shopped. It was easy enough to get by, but even so, every day we came across something that was new to us.

When we visited the local park, I was amazed at the way people treated their dogs. They were well cared for and people played games with them. Back in our village, no one had taken much notice of dogs. They were scruffy, mangy things. There, only the important animals – the buffaloes and goats – were well looked after.

It took a while to get used to the new house, too. It seemed exotic with its heating system and the gleaming new bathroom and toilet. It was such a luxury to stand for ages under a shower with an endless supply of hot water, to put clothes into a washing machine and not have to help Ammi wash everything by hand.

Baba took us on the Underground one day. Poor Ammi sat rigidly in her seat wearing the same expression of terror she'd had on the aeroplane.

'Where are we going?' she whispered to me, over and over.

'Down to the middle of the earth,' said Imran, who had come with us.

Ammi's hand flew to her mouth.

I laughed. 'He's teasing you, Ammi,' I said, but her terrified look didn't clear until we came out into the daylight again.

As Asma and I began to get more used to our surroundings, the boys' constant boasting became more and more irritating.

'They think they know it all,' I said to Asma. 'I wish they'd stop showing off.'

She squeezed my hand. 'Don't worry, little sister. We'll show them. We'll soon speak English much better than they do.'

Ammi let us watch much more television than she had back in our village.

Khalil said it was because she couldn't understand what the people were saying – and I think he was right. One day Asma and I watched a rather rude play. We could follow the sense of it and both of us were shocked, but we didn't switch it off because Ammi was sitting with us, smiling and nodding. She hadn't a clue what the actors were saying, but she loved the beautiful dresses!

September came, and it was time to start school. I had one more year in primary school and then I would join Asma at the all-girls secondary school.

I didn't sleep a wink the night before the start of term, and in the morning I felt so sick that I couldn't eat any breakfast.

Three of my cousins came to fetch me; they all went to the same school.

'Cheer up, Halima,' said one of them. 'It's OK. You'll be fine.'

'We were all nervous at first,' said another.

I was grateful for their kindness, but they'd been living in England for years. They already spoke good English when they started school. I felt the tears welling up.

'I won't be able to follow what the teachers are saying,' I blurted out.

'Yes you will,' said the first cousin. 'The teachers are used to people not speaking good English. There are lots of kids like you who've just come from Pakistan and lots of the teachers speak several languages. Don't worry.'

The walk to school took only a few minutes, but I wanted it to last for ever. I didn't want to arrive, to be flung into this new and frightening life. I stared down at the pavement and concentrated on the little sparkling bits in the paving slabs that glistened from the recent rain. And although the streets were familiar to me by then, it was as if I was seeing them for the first time with their muddle of houses and the litter blown by the wind into the tiny front gardens.

And then we were there, walking through the gates into the yard where all the pupils were gathered together, mostly in small groups, talking and shouting or playing. I kept close by my cousins, trying to make myself invisible, and I thought longingly of the little dusty primary school back in my village.

Even with my cousins to help me, I found the first week very confusing. It was a big school with over thirty of us in each class – girls and boys – and they were noisy and disrespectful to the teachers. They should bring the village elders over here to sort them out, I thought.

To begin with, I stuck with my cousins, but I could see they were getting fed up with me. I didn't blame them. They had their own friends and they didn't want to be lumbered with me all the time.

My cousins and I were always dressed in our traditional *salwaar kameez* with a hijab covering our hair, but some of the other Pakistani girls wore Western clothes and wore no head covering at all.

'Why aren't you covered?' I asked one of them.

She shrugged. 'My family don't believe in all that,' she said. "We don't go to the mosque or anything.'

I was shocked. 'But you are a Muslim?'

'Sort of,' she said. 'But all that stuff's so boring.'

I had never heard my religion being spoken of in that way. I was horrified and wondered whether God would strike her down immediately, but nothing happened and I watched her skip off without a care in the world.

Tentatively, I began to make a few friends – Pakistani girls at first, but then, gradually, some English girls too. The teachers mixed us up a lot, so I'd often find myself working on something with an English girl, and that forced me to speak English.

It was surprising how quickly both Asma and I adjusted and how quickly our English improved. We had no choice; all the lessons were in English and we were conscious, all the time, of Baba's determination that we should do well.

'How was school?' he would ask every evening. 'What did you learn?'

Sometimes I would answer him in English. I thought he would be pleased, but he got angry.

'Disrespectful girl!' he said in Pushtu. 'Speak so that your mother can understand you!'

'I thought you wanted us all to learn English,' I muttered.

'Don't you dare answer back,' he said, scowling at me.

I looked across at Asma, but she pretended not be listening.

'Why does he get so cross when we speak English at home?' I asked her, when we were alone.

Asma looked at her nails. 'He doesn't speak English too well, Halima. I don't think he wants us to show him up.'

I stared at her. 'But he keeps going on about us getting a good education. He could learn better English if we spoke at home. We could teach him.'

But even as I said that, I knew how stupid it sounded. Asma laughed.

'Us teach him, Halima? What about his pride?'

☪ ☪ ☪

Little by little, we all settled into our new routines and in no time it was nearly the end of my first term. Everything to do with Christmas fascinated me.

So many advertisements on the TV, so many decorations in the shops, and everyone spending money buying presents.

I knew a bit about Christmas from watching television in Pakistan, but nothing had prepared me for the endless talk about it, the constant pressure to buy presents, to spend more and more money.

Some of my non-Muslim friends bought me little presents. I felt a bit embarrassed about it, so I asked Ammi for money to buy them something in return.

She was shocked. 'We don't celebrate Christmas, Halima. What are you thinking of?'

I looked at her and scowled. 'Surely I should give them something if they give me something?'

Ammi looked uncomfortable. 'You must explain about being Muslim,' she mumbled.

'They know I'm a Muslim,' I said crossly. 'But everyone celebrates Christmas here. I don't want to be different.'

In the end it wasn't difficult. Most of my non-Muslim friends understood and weren't bothered.

'We just give presents at Christmas to people we like,' said one friend. 'It's no big deal.'

I felt happy. I was accepted. Other girls liked me.

And so the new year began and I started to feel more and more a part of my surroundings. Although the primary school didn't have many facilities for playing sport, I had a natural talent for gymnastics, despite being short and stocky.

'Look at Halima!' shouted my cousins, as I did handstands and cartwheels or scrambled up the climbing bars. 'She's like a little monkey!'

I was a fast runner, too. Chasing after Imran in the village had been good training. I would race round the playground at break time, easily outstripping my classmates as we played noisy games which usually ended in breathless giggles. And my English was getting better and better.

But while Asma and I had settled well at our schools and our English was improving all the time, poor Ammi made no progress. She spent all her time with her relations and only went to shops where they understood Pushtu or Urdu.

By the following September, when I moved to the secondary school to be with Asma, I was already growing away from Ammi. She knew it, too, and sometimes she looked longingly at me, searching for a glimpse of that little girl who had once been so dependent on her. Now she depended on me to translate English words for her when she couldn't understand.

But we still did our embroidery together. Here, at least, she could still teach me something, and I always tried to spend some time each day working on it with her. We would chat happily together, remembering the cousins and aunties back in the village who were always laughing and gossiping as they sewed, sitting in someone's house or outside under a shady tree.

'Do you remember that special *dupatta* I made for your cousin's wedding?' said Ammi, her head bent and her small, delicate fingers sewing tiny stitches to make an intricate pattern on a bodice.

I was embroidering the sleeves which would be sewn into the bodice, and I took my eyes off my own work and sat back and stretched. 'Of course I remember,' I said. 'It was so beautiful. That deep red chiffon – and all those sequins and beads!'

Ammi's hands were still for a moment and there was a dreamy look in her eyes. I knew she was thinking of the village.

'Will you make *dupattas* for us, Ammi? For me and Asma, when we get married?'

She focused on me again, and smiled. 'Of course, Halima. When the time comes.'

She took my piece of work from me and inspected it critically before she handed it back.

'You already sew beautifully,' she said softly. 'By the time your wedding comes, you will be better than me. You will be able to make your own *dupatta*.'

CHAPTER SIX

Starting at secondary school wasn't half as bad as starting primary school. Lots of my friends and relations came with me, I already knew some of Asma's friends, and my English was good. I felt much happier and more confident.

And on the very first day, I met Kate.

Kate. How can I describe her? Wild, clever, Irish and as fair as I was dark. Always questioning everything, her green eyes darting this way and that and her loud raucous laugh breaking into every conversation.

When I first met her, I was shocked at her frankness. But I felt challenged by it, too.

'You never stop banging on about your precious village in Pakistan, Halima, so why did you come here?'

'I had no choice,' I retorted. 'My father brought us over.'

'What for? So you could get a free education?'

I bridled. 'Well yes, I suppose so. Schools are better here.'

‘OK, so you work hard, you get your good English education, then what will you do? Get married and go back to your village?’

‘No. I want to go to college. And then… I don’t know, I haven’t really thought about it.’

‘You should learn to think, Halima. That’s what you’re at school for.’ Then she laughed and I joined in. It was impossible to take offence.

But her constant challenges got to me. Now that my English was better, I started to read English newspapers, to try and understand what was going on in the world and how people thought in England.

Baba caught me reading one at home. He tore it out of my hands.

‘What are you doing with that rubbish?’ he shouted.

‘It’s not rubbish,’ I muttered.

‘What did you say?’

‘I said, it is not rubbish,’ I shouted.

He held the front page under my nose. ‘Look!’ he screamed. ‘Look at this woman on the front page. It is immodest! Is that what you want to become?’

‘Baba,’ I said, laughing in spite of my anger. ‘She’s wearing a low-cut top, that’s all. And she’s a politician, for goodness sake. An MP! You know – a well-educated woman – the sort of woman you want me to be!’

He scrunched up the paper and hurled it on the floor, then marched out of the room slamming the door behind him.

I bent down, picked up the paper and smoothed down the front page, shaking my head in frustration. Perhaps I would become a politician. That would show him!

If Baba thought this incident would put me off reading the English papers, he was wrong, but after that, if I brought any home with me I made sure he never found them. And they gave me ammunition to use in my arguments with Kate. We argued about everything, but particularly about Islam.

'You don't understand our ways,' I said to her once, exasperated at some joke she'd made at my expense.

'Then take me back home and introduce me to your family,' she said. 'How can I understand where you're coming from if you don't let me meet your family?'

So I took her up on it. I invited her over for a meal after school.

Ammi was nervous.

'She won't speak my language, Halima. And she won't like our food.'

'She's my best friend, Ammi, and she wants to meet you all,' I said. 'Don't worry, she'll love you and she'll eat whatever you give her.'

But it wasn't a great success. Although I'd often

'Why not. Why shouldn't I?'

Asma picked at some loose cotton threads on her top. 'Think of the future, little sister.'

'What do you mean?' I said sulkily, although I knew what was coming.

'You know that Baba will arrange a marriage for me – and for you, too, when your turn comes. Don't be too influenced by girls like Kate. Being too independent could get you into trouble. Be careful.'

I didn't answer. Nothing was going to stop me being friendly with Kate, so I kept quiet.

We progressed up the school, Kate and I. I had many other friends, Muslim and non-Muslim, and I was happy there. At first I struggled a bit with the language but it wasn't long before I was fluent in English. I was learning so much – not just school work but about the world, about different points of view. And I was reading. Not just newspapers but loads of books.

Kate read all the time, too. Sometimes she would toss a book at me.

'Here, read this, Halima. This'll open your eyes!'

Sometimes we would talk about books. Usually our views were totally at odds and we would disagree about everything but somehow that didn't matter. It was stimulating and it made me think, sharpened my wits, distilled my views.

Kate wasn't the only person I disagreed with. Even within the Muslim community at school there were disagreements. Some girls came from much more liberal families than mine. Some never even went near the mosque. As I became more confident, I would challenge these girls about their way of life. Not that it got me anywhere; they usually shrugged and turned away.

One day our English teacher, Miss Brunner, asked me to stay behind after her lesson.

'I'm setting up a debating society, Halima, and I'd really like you to join it. You speak well and you can put over your views. Why don't you come along? I think you'd enjoy it.'

So I began going along after school. It was here that I learnt to defend my own point of view, but it was also where I really began to listen to others.

'My head's bursting,' I said to Kate one day. 'So many different sides. So many different opinions. How can we ever agree about anything?'

'Ha!' said Kate. 'So you admit you might be wrong about some things.'

'No! Not about important things.'

But it was true that I was less sure. I was questioning everything.

CHAPTER SEVEN

Kate

Halima thinks I'm so sure of myself, so confident. But it's not true. I've learnt to keep myself apart and not form attachments. That way, you don't get hurt. I had a tough protective shell around me when I first met her and she's the first person who's cracked it.

I met Halima on our first day at secondary school. My family had just come to London and I didn't know a soul. My dad goes from one job to another so we're always moving around, but my mum said that this is the final move. We're in London for good – or so she says. But she's said that before and they always quarrel about it. I'm sick of their rows.

Anyway, there I was, pretending to be cool and confident but feeling like shit inside, scowling at everyone, when I saw Halima chatting to a group of other Muslim girls. You can always spot them; they have to wear the school uniform – at least the trousers – but they are allowed to wear those hideous scarves over their heads.

No good expecting that lot to make friends,

I thought to myself. I was about to turn away, when Halima looked up and caught my eye. And smiled at me.

I was so grateful that I walked right over and said, 'Hi.'

She had a funny face. Not beautiful exactly, but strong and full of character. She was quite short and her hips were a bit on the chunky side.

'I'm Kate,' I said.

'I'm Halima,' she said.

And then we both laughed.

There I was, this great, tall, pale Irish girl with ghastly red hair flying about everywhere, and there was she, this dumpy, dark little Muslim. We made a strange pair. And immediately we both saw it.

I've never been one for beating about the bush. 'I've never spoken to a Muslim before,' I said, expecting her to clam up.

She didn't. She tossed my remark right back at me.

'And I've never spoken to a redhead before,' she retorted.

And we laughed again.

So that's how it began, this unlikely friendship.

If I thought she'd be angry when I questioned her faith and her way of life, I was right. But not in an over-emotional way. She knows where she's coming from. She always defends it and she's much more sure of herself than I am, though I would never let her think that.

I was really curious about her background and I pestered her to invite me over.

Well! That was an eye-opener! The inside of her little terraced house was a shrine to Pakistan. Glittery cushions, floaty chiffon and bits of silk, ornaments everywhere. So different from my home.

I could tell that her mum was uneasy as soon as I went through the door. She didn't speak a word of English, so Halima had to translate for her. But she smiled a lot and she had prepared the most amazing meal. I'd already met Halima's sister, Asma, because she's at school with us. She couldn't be more different from Halima. She's very slim and her skin is a stunning pale brown. She has long tapering fingers and toes and a stillness about her. I think she'd drive men wild, though I guess she's not allowed to do much of that, coming from the family she does!

But I'd not met the brothers before.

I went up to the older one, Khalil. 'Hi, I'm Kate. Halima's friend from school.'

He looked as if I'd molested him. He blushed and muttered something.

Imran was much more friendly. But the way the boys treated their sisters and their mother was appalling.

At dinner, they let the women do all the work. They didn't lift a finger. I offered to help clear the meal away but the other women refused to let me.

'You are our guest,' said Asma.

Although Asma was friendly enough, I sensed a bit of a freeze there. I don't think she really approves of me being such a mate of Halima's.

I turned to the boys, who were lounging about on chairs talking to each other, ignoring me.

'Shouldn't you give you mother some help?' I said, all innocent.

Imran looked at me pityingly. 'That's women's work, Kate,' he said, as if he was explaining something to a slow-witted two-year-old.

It took me a moment to pick my jaw up off the floor, and I was just about to start a serious argument with these idlers when Halima came into the room again and I caught her eye. I bit back my comments. I really wanted to take issue with the boys but I could see she wanted to keep the peace.

When we met at school the next day, I let fly about her brothers. I think I overdid it, because she was really angry with me that time. I know she agrees with me in her heart, but family means a lot to her. She won't have anything said against them.

It took us a day or two to get back on track again after that – and I didn't get any more invitations.

CHAPTER EIGHT

Halima

Gradually, things changed at home. I was so used to speaking English at school that I found it hard to speak Pushtu at home. Sometimes I broke into English without realising it.

'Have some respect for your mother,' shouted Baba. 'Speak in Pushtu.'

One day I shouted back at him. 'We're living in England, Baba. She should learn to speak the language.' And then I muttered in English, 'And so should you.'

I thought he hadn't heard me, but he had.

'Disrespectful girl. Go to your room. How dare you!'

I sighed and went off. It was easier that way.

It was about that time that I found a Saturday morning job in a dress shop near our house. I thought that Baba might try and stop me working there but, surprisingly, he agreed.

'Good. Good, Halima,' he said vaguely. 'It will

improve your English and you will save a little money.'

I had been anticipating a fight and I was amazed. He must have been in a good mood that day. Or perhaps he was relieved that I'd be out of his way on a Saturday.

I was growing apart from my parents. Although I still loved Ammi and appreciated all she had tried to instil into us children, my horizons were much broader than hers. I was beginning to think differently. I was restless and uncertain of what I wanted. As for my father, what little respect I had had for him had melted away. For Ammi's sake I tried to toe the line, but I found it harder and harder to obey him.

Fortunately, Baba soon forgot about my insolence. He had a bigger problem – a problem with Imran.

Imran, the spoilt favourite, the clever one, the charmer, the golden boy. Baba had such high hopes of him. Imran was bright and popular, but Baba kept putting the pressure on him. Being second was never good enough. He must always be top of his class. He must make the family proud of him.

At first, the rows between Baba and Imran were no big deal. Baba would berate him for not achieving high marks, Imran would shrug and go out, slamming the door behind him. The next day, it was as if nothing had happened.

But it went on and on. Day after day, Baba would be on at him.

'You have the best brains in the family, you silly boy. You are wasting them. What are you doing with your time, eh? You are not studying seriously. I know you are not.'

One dreadful day, I had just got back from school and let myself into the house and I heard terrible shouting going on in the front room. I stood uncertainly in the hall, not knowing whether to creep past or stay where I was. The two of them were yelling at each other.

'Get off my back, Baba! If you go on like this, I'll quit school altogether. Just leave me alone!'

'But Imran, you know what plans I have for you. You will be a lawyer, maybe, or an accountant. You have the brains, son. You must make your family proud of you.'

Then Imran completely lost it. I'd never heard him use swear words before, but they all came tumbling out.

'The family. Always the bloody family. What about me? And what the hell do you know about study, eh? What studying have you ever done? You work in a dead end job surrounded by your relations. You've been living here for years and you hardly speak a word of English, for God's sake! So don't lecture me about studying.'

'Imran!'

'Get stuffed. You're doing my head in, going on at me all the time. What if I don't want to be a bloody lawyer or accountant, eh? Have you ever bothered to ask what I really want to do? Have you?'

'I have sacrificed everything for you,' shouted Baba. 'I have worked here for years so you can come here and have a good education. Now you throw all this back in my face.'

'Just stop going on at me. I'm not some sort of genius. Why don't you preach at Khalil for a change?'

'Khalil is not as clever. You are the one from whom I expect the most.'

'Too bloody bad! I'm not going to fit in with your plans any more. They're your plans, not mine.'

There was a sudden silence and then a shuffling noise. Then a sharp intake of breath, a thump and a scream.

I knew that sound and my heart raced. Sometimes Baba hit me if I disobeyed or angered him. But I was sure he had never hit Imran before.

The door of the front room opened and Imran staggered out. He was clutching his shoulder and sobbing. He saw me, and turned his face away as he ran upstairs to his room.

Through the open door I could see that Baba had his hands over his eyes and his back to me. Very quietly, unnoticed, I slid past the door and followed Imran upstairs.

I knocked on his door.

'It's only me.'

'Go away.'

I took no notice and went into his bedroom. I said nothing, just sat down on the edge of his bed. He was facing the wall and he wouldn't look round.

'Imran.'

'Shut up. Go away!'

I stayed where I was. I creased the duvet cover between my finger and thumb.

'It's not fair, the way he keeps getting at you, Imran,' I muttered. 'He just doesn't understand.'

Slowly Imran swivelled round to look at me. His face was blotched with tears. I reached out for his hand and he let me take it. He sniffed. 'Little sister,' he said.

We didn't speak for a while, then Imran said. 'It's eating me up, Halima. Every day. Every day he questions me about my marks, where I've been, what I've been doing, why I'm not top. I tell you, I can't stand it much longer. It's stifling. This house is stifling, the family is stifling and all the bloody cousins and aunties and uncles. I need to get out. I need to be free of them.'

'You wouldn't leave us,' I said, shocked. 'You wouldn't really leave us, Imran?'

Imran shrugged. Then he smiled at me. 'I don't want to leave Ammi and you and Asma – and even boring old Khalil – but I can't stay in the house with Baba. He just doesn't understand what he's doing to me.'

It will pass, I thought, as I made my way back to the room I shared with Asma and slid my school bag off my back. I took out some books and started on my homework. A little later, Ammi brought me a drink.

'Did you hear Baba and Imran shouting at each other?' I asked her.

She looked worried for a moment, then put her hand on my shoulder. 'They'll make it up,' she said. 'Imran loves his Baba.'

'Baba should be careful,' I said. 'He's pushing Imran too hard.'

Ammi's jaw set and she frowned. I knew that expression well. 'Don't criticise your father,' she said. 'He knows what he's doing.'

'But he's never had to study, Ammi. He doesn't...'

'Enough, Halima!'

I sighed and went back to my work. Couldn't Ammi see what was happening? Couldn't she feel the atmosphere in the place? Imran, the light-hearted one, the star of the family, always teasing and joking, was becoming moody and silent.

When I talked to Asma about it, she didn't seem too worried.

'Huh! All teenage boys are moody, Halima. It comes with the territory.'

But it was more than that.

During the next few days, Baba and Imran hardly spoke to each other. The rest of us tiptoed round them, trying not to rock the boat. Khalil always seemed to say the wrong thing, though. He either made some heavy-handed joke or he banged on about what he'd been doing at school and then got his head bitten off either by Baba or Imran. Poor Khalil. I know he was only trying to help, but I despaired of him. He simply didn't know the meaning of the word 'tact'.

What an idiot, I thought.

But it turned out that the rest of us had been just as blind as Khalil. None of us saw it coming.

About two weeks after I'd heard the screaming match between Baba and Imran, Imran disappeared.

Quietly, he had been making his plans. He left very little behind and his room was clean and tidy. Somehow, this made it worse. Imran, who had always been untidy and whose room had always been such a tip. It was unnatural.

Ammi found the note. I was the only other person in the house at the time and I heard her cry out. I ran along the passage and into Imram's room. Ammi was standing by the bed, holding a piece of paper.

'Read it, Halima. Read it for me!'

I took it, wondering, even as I did so, why on earth he'd written it in English.

And then, as I read, I understood. The note said a lot of harsh things about Baba, things he wouldn't have wanted Ammi to hear. I told her what she needed to know.

'He's safe, Ammi,' I said quietly. 'He's gone to live with a school friend.'

'Who? Who is he living with?' She was standing in front of me, tears welling up in her big dark eyes, twisting a sodden tissue in her hand.

'He doesn't say. Another Pakistani family,' I said.

'Oh Imran,' she wailed. 'Oh the disgrace, Halima. How has it come to this?'

I took her by the shoulders. 'It's not your fault, Ammi. Please don't blame yourself.'

'How can I tell Baba?'

I shrugged. 'You must tell him the truth, Ammi. Tell him that he has driven his favourite son away.'

In her fury, Ammi struck out, her arms flailing in the air. 'NO! Don't be ridiculous, child. Baba has done everything for him. He has worked so hard to earn money for you all. How can you say that, Halima!'

I didn't answer. I felt so sad as I watched her fighting to control herself. How could she understand that, in bringing his children here to England, Baba was losing them. Our minds were expanding while his – and hers – were shrinking.

As I stood helplessly by, I wondered at their refusal to move on. It seemed to me that we had become fossilised. We were clinging on to the life we had known back in Pakistan, to all the customs, all the rules. It was a sort of security blanket.

And yet, when we'd been back to our village – twice, since we'd been in England – I sensed that things had loosened up there. Talking to my cousins there, it seemed that they had more freedom than in the old days. They told me that the attitude of the elders had become a little more liberal.

The village elders may have become more liberal. But Baba had certainly not.

At first, when he heard what had happened, he shut himself away and refused to speak to anyone. And then came the fury: shouting against Imran, railing at the rest of us.

'That boy is no longer my son!' he shouted. 'He has disgraced us. How dare he leave us. Doesn't he understand what he's doing to our family honour?'

Ammi tried to placate him. 'Perhaps he will come home, Baba. Perhaps, when he has calmed down, he will return.'

Baba was even more angry then. I could see the spittle gathering at the edge of his lips as he spat out his reply.

'Don't be so foolish, woman. Do you think I would ever let him in this house again, after what he has done to us?'

Imran's absence left a great yawning void in our family and it had an effect on us all. Khalil tried to curry favour by being a model son and was ignored or snapped at for his trouble. Ammi, Asma and I kept our heads well below the parapet, and Baba became even more bad-tempered and despotic.

CHAPTER NINE

And Baba was becoming ever more watchful, particularly of Asma and me.

We had nothing to hide, but the questioning grew more oppressive.

'Why are you late back from school, Halima?' He was standing by the front door, waiting for me, tapping his watch with his finger.

'It's Wednesday, Baba. You know that I go to the debating society on Wednesdays after school.'

I tried to push past him into the house, but he didn't move. He folded his arms.

'Huh! Debating! What is debating?'

I sighed. I was practised in answering these sorts of questions. 'Learning to put forward my point of view, Baba. Learning to put forward the Muslim point of view to unbelievers.' Of course, this was only partly true, but it was an answer Baba couldn't challenge. Sulkily he let me into the house.

And Asma was getting even more scrutiny. Even Baba couldn't ignore the fact that she was growing into a beautiful young woman. There was no doubt that she had had all the luck when good looks had been handed out. I was OK, but I had big hips and a hooked nose – Baba's features – whereas Asma had Ammi's delicate bones and chiselled features.

One evening, as we were all eating together, Baba leaned back in his chair and smiled at Asma. We had just heard that she had been accepted at university. There was no question of leaving home, so she had only applied to London colleges, and she'd had several offers.

The first of his family to have further education! Baba was so proud of her, though of course he didn't show it.

'Now, Asma, we must start to look for a husband for you,' he announced.

Asma stopped eating and looked up at him. She said nothing, but I could see the fear in her eyes. Did this mean she wouldn't be allowed to go to college? If she wasn't allowed to go, then I wouldn't be, either. I held my breath.

Baba picked at his teeth for ages before he spoke again. 'Yes,' he said, at last, 'We must start looking now, and then the wedding will take place as soon as you have finished your studies.'

I could see the tension in Asma's face. A tiny vein throbbed at her temple. She swallowed.

'You mean my school studies?' she asked quietly.

Baba laughed. 'No, silly girl. Your university studies, of course. You will marry as soon as you are through college.'

Asma smiled with relief.

'Isn't that very late?' asked Ammi, quietly. 'She will be quite old.'

Baba scowled. 'It is different here, Ammi. Surely you understand that by now? Women are expected to have a good education.'

I said nothing, but I was relieved. I wanted to go to college, too, and I certainly didn't want to get married at eighteen.

During the next few months, Baba busied himself finding a suitable husband for Asma.

When I mentioned this to Kate, she was horrified.

'Halima, that is gross! How can she let your father choose her husband for her?'

Half of me agreed, but I wasn't going to let Kate get away with it.

'And is your way any better?' I said.

'Well, at least we get to choose who we want to marry.'

'So do we,' I said. 'Our parents help, that's all. They find a boy with the same background, the same education, and then they introduce him to the girl. What's wrong with that?'

'So Asma can say no if she doesn't like the man?'

I nodded. In theory, this was true, though I knew that Baba would be furious if she rejected his choice.

Kate went on. 'Your family's different, then, from these girls at school who disappear at fourteen and get taken home to Pakistan and married off?'

'Yes. Yes, of course. My parents would never do that.'

The previous summer term, the school had lost several Muslim girls. They had simply left at the end of term and never returned. Or they came back married and then had to help save up to bring their husband over to England.

Kate had something to say about these girls. 'So they're just providing a man with a ticket to come to this country – is that it?'

I shrugged. 'It's not that simple, Kate.'

'Looks pretty simple to me. It's all about getting a job for a bloke in the West, isn't it?'

'No. Not always. It's complicated. It's about families. It's about who is suitable to marry whom. It's about who has land, who has not.'

Kate had been trying to twist her wild curls into a rubber band. She gave up and let it all hang loose again. Then she turned to face me.

'How can these kids agree to it, Halima?'

'To what?'

'How can they cave in like that? They're happy at school, and then suddenly they're whisked away to marry a stranger in Pakistan. Don't some of them object?'

Suddenly I felt cross with her. Compared to the families of some of these girls, my family were positively liberal. I'd known many of them and I'd talked over their situation with them. I understood their predicament and I also understood why they did as they were told.

'Yes, of course they can object, but just think it through, Kate. Think of the consequences.'

'What do you mean?'

'If they don't do as they're told, their families will force them to do it anyway.'

Kate frowned. 'How can you force someone to do something against their will?'

I sighed, trying to be patient with her. 'It's about family honour, Kate. If a girl refuses, she is dishonouring her family.'

'So?'

'It's really, really important to us. If you dishonour your family, they will disown you or, worse, they may even kidnap you and force you to do as they wish. A brother or a father or some other family member will physically force you.'

'But in this day and age, Halima, how can that happen? The law...'

I laughed. 'The law! Believe me, Kate, in some families, their own law is more powerful than the law of the land.'

She stared at me and I went on. 'Going against your family's wishes means you may never see them again,' I said quietly.

Kate was silent for a moment, as my words sank in. Then, 'You still have no contact with Imran?'

I picked up her rubber band and started to force her strands of hair into it. 'He texts Asma and me – and sometimes he rings us on our mobiles.'

'Then you know where he is?'

I shook my head. 'No. He never says.'

Finally, I arranged her unruly mop into some kind of order. 'He's left school and got some dead-end job.'

'That's sad. He was so bright.'

'Yeah.' I dropped my hand and she caught it and squeezed it.

'You miss him, don't you?'

Kate wasn't usually touchy-feely, and this out-of-character gesture caught me unawares. I burst into tears.

'Hey, Halima. Don't cry. Please don't cry!'

I drew my hand away from hers and sniffed and

blew my nose. 'I wish I could see him,' I said.

'Why can't you?'

'I've asked if we can meet, but he won't let me. He's protecting me.'

'Protecting you?'

I nodded. 'If I met up with him, Kate, someone would see us. However careful we were, someone would see us. And they'd tell my parents and then there'd be terrible rows and I'd be grounded.'

'God,' said Kate, shocked. 'How heavy is that?'

'I know. I know it's hard for you to understand. But it's how things are with us.'

Not long after this conversation, I persuaded Kate to join the after-school debating club. She took to it like a duck to water.

'Hey,' she said, after one session. 'I'm really enjoying this.' She nudged me. 'And I'm seeing a different side to you, too!'

I knew what she meant. In some ways, the debating club was keeping me sane. The members were bright and they all had strong opinions – often radically opposed to one another – and in this atmosphere I felt able to express opinions I'd never be able to air at home, discuss them, toss them around, listen to others' views. Debates were often heated, but Miss Brunner always kept the lid on things and summed up the conclusions in a balanced way, and I always left feeling stretched and tipped a little out of my comfort zone.

She was my ideal, Miss Brunner. Here was a young woman, highly educated, attractive, her own person, shaping the thoughts and expanding the minds of all these girls from such different backgrounds.

Sometimes I stayed on a little, helping her to clear up. She asked me about my family once and I told her all about Imran and about Baba's search for a husband for Asma. She kept her opinions to herself, she was never judgemental and, over the months, I came to know her well. I felt that she was the one adult I could trust completely.

CHAPTER TEN

Asma did well at university. She was Baba's perfect daughter.

Like everyone else, I loved my sister and I envied her effortless charm. Sometimes I wished I could be more like her, not just in looks, but in temperament.

'Are you happy?' I asked her once, as we were getting ready for bed.

'What sort of question is that?'

I shrugged. 'Well, are you happy that Baba's going to find a husband for you? What if you don't like him? What if he's old and fat and ugly?'

She smiled. 'If he's old and fat and ugly, Baba won't introduce him to me.'

'Or he might be cruel. He might keep you under his thumb, not let you do the things you want to do.'

'Oh shut up, Halima. Let's wait and see, shall we?'

In fact, Baba went to a lot of trouble to find the right man for Asma. He knew that he held some trump cards. Asma was intelligent, beautiful and modest, and she came from a respected Pushtoon family who owned land back in Pakistan.

There was, of course, a skeleton in our cupboard – Imran – but his disappearance was never mentioned. Baba kept hidden our family's disgrace.

Negotiations began in earnest as Asma entered her final year at college.

And then one evening, Baba came home full of excitement.

'Asma, come here, child. I think we have found a husband for you.'

Asma sat at Baba's feet as he described the young man to her, and the rest of us listened, too.

A photo was produced and passed around. I scrutinised it carefully. He was good-looking and there were laughter lines round his eyes, which was a good sign. If he took up with our family, he'd certainly need a sense of humour! Also, his family had lived in England for two generations and he had been born here so, with luck, he wouldn't be too overbearing as a husband.

Asma handed the photo back. She smiled. 'He looks nice, Baba,' she said. 'What's his name?'

Baba rubbed his hands together. 'Habib. He has seen your photo, Asma, and he wants to come and visit.'

Hardly surprising, I thought. Anyone seeing Asma's photo would rush to meet her.

Baba went on. 'He's got a good job. A nice flat. Good family.'

I drifted off into my own thoughts as Baba banged on about the virtues of his prospective son-in-law. Clearly Baba had set his heart on this young man. I just hoped he was as nice as Baba thought he was.

And when my turn came, what would happen? Who would Baba find for me? Suddenly, this didn't seem so far away.

Baba clapped his hands and I dragged my thoughts back to the present.

'Halima. Pay attention! We have invited Habib and his parents to come and see us next Thursday evening. The whole family must be here to greet him.'

The whole family? I thought. What about Imran?

The next few days went by in a whirl. Ammi and the aunties chatted on the phone or visited each other all the time and when Thursday arrived, Baba, Ammi, Khalil and I were all lined up to meet Habib and his family. Asma stayed in her room. She would make a brief appearance later, when Habib's family and my family had had a chance to get to know each other.

The moment that Habib walked through the door, I knew he would be kind to Asma. I can't explain why; it was the way he walked, his relaxed attitude, the way he smiled. I let out a huge sigh of relief. This man was OK. I just hoped he wouldn't be too put off by our family.

But, amazingly, his family seemed immediately at home with us. Habib's mother and Ammi never stopped chatting, his father smiled broadly at Baba and embraced him, and Habib talked to Khalil and me naturally.

Then, after about half an hour, Asma made her entrance, bringing in tea and cakes.

Everyone stopped talking and turned to look. I felt so proud of her. She never faltered, gracefully acknowledging the visitors and then sitting down to serve the tea. I was watching Habib closely; his whole face lit up when he saw her; it was obvious she had made a good impression. But how could she not? It was impossible not to love my sister.

I sat beside Asma and helped her serve out the tea and cakes, and Habib was close by. He spoke gently to her, asking one or two questions, making a few jokes, eating everything she handed to him.

At last, Habib and his parents left. They were hardly out of the door before we all started talking at once.

Ammi hugged Asma. 'What a lovely boy!' she said, over and over.

'Well, What do you think, Asma?' asked Baba.

'I liked him. I liked him very much, Baba.'

'So did I,' said Khalil. 'He's a good bloke.'

Baba rubbed his hands together. 'And he liked you,

Asma. He liked you very, very much. I could tell. Oh yes, very much. Undoubtedly, we shall have a *magni.*'

The very next day, Habib's father sent the proposal to Baba, and it didn't take Asma and the rest of us long to make up our minds. We had a simple *magni* ceremony a few weeks later to formally seal the engagement and the *shadi* date was set for the end of the academic year, when Asma finished at college.

I told Kate all about it. I was nervous of her reaction.

But Kate was thoughtful. 'So, you really think it was love at first sight, eh?'

'Well not love, exactly, but they were attracted to each other, certainly, and he's a really nice guy, Kate.'

'How do you know? You only saw him for an hour.'

'I just do. He was easy-going and intelligent. And our families got on well.'

'Ah. The families!'

'Kate, you know how important that is to us.'

'Sure. So what happens now? Do they get to sleep together, to see if that's all going to work, too!'

I laughed. 'No – Baba would kill her if she did that. But they'll get to hang out together, get to know each other a bit before the *shadi.*'

'So, is it going to be one of these vast Asian weddings, then?'

I nodded. 'Big. But not as big as it would have

been back home in Pakistan.'

Ammi was disappointed about that. She so much wanted to go back to our village and have the wedding there, but Habib's family were all in London and they had access to a place where we could hold the big parties.

'Never mind, Ammi,' said Asma. 'Maybe Khalil's wedding will be in Pakistan. Or Halima's.'

Baba looked across at me. 'Oh yes, certainly. Halima's wedding will be in Pakistan.'

I frowned, wondering why he'd said that. But I soon forgot his chance remark and was swept up in plans for the wedding.

From the day of the *magni*, Ammi and all the aunties and friends went into overdrive. Every time I came home from school there were crowds of them in the house poring over recipes, inspecting swatches of fabric. And always the constant chatter and laughter.

Poor Asma. Ammi and the aunties seemed to forget that she was studying for her finals. To them, her exams were utterly unimportant compared to her wedding. Sometimes, in the evening, when we were both in our room studying, Ammi or one of the aunties would barge in and insist we came and gave an opinion on this or that.

Our bedroom had always been big enough for the two of us, but now it was cluttered with wedding stuff.

Asma felt bad about it.

'You could always move into Imran's room, Halima,' she said. 'if you want a bit of space.'

I shook my head. 'I'll soon have this room to myself. And anyway, I don't want to move into his room. It's his. We should leave it in case he comes home.'

We both knew that this wouldn't happen, and Asma gave me a quizzical look.

I tried to explain. 'If I did use his room, it would be like saying he's never going to come back, never going to be part of the family again.'

Asma sighed. 'It's sad he won't be at my wedding.'

But there was no possibility of that. As far as Baba was concerned, Imran no longer existed.

CHAPTER ELEVEN

Perhaps Asma's wedding wasn't quite how Ammi had imagined the wedding of her first daughter. Back in our village, it would have gone on for a week, but, even though it wasn't in Pakistan, it was pretty special and we spread it out over four days instead.

To begin with, there was all the beauty preparation. Asma had a special facial and body massage and spent hours at the hairdresser. Then, dressed in yellow, she was brought into the front room under a big scarf held up by Khalil and me and a few of our London cousins, where she received all her family.

This was our family party. Habib had a party with his family.

The next event was the *mehndi*. On this day Habib's family presented Asma with her wedding dress. Again, the parties were separate. Ours was a really big family party, this time with all the cousins and aunties and uncles, some of whom had flown in specially from Pakistan. We had lots of music – banging drums and lots of dancing and endless good things to eat at the buffet – *tikkas, naan, biryani,* curries. Everyone was brightly dressed and Asma had her hands beautifully painted with henna patterns.

The actual marriage ceremony took place on the third day. Asma's dress was of traditional red, very elaborate, with a *dupatta* – a veil – and she wore heavy jewellery. Habib wore an embroidered suit and a special turban. They made a handsome couple as they sat together on a stage at the end of the room.

The last event of the wedding was the *valmina,* where the marriage was announced to everyone. I was allowed to invite a few friends to this. Asma was a bit dubious when I suggested Kate.

'She's my best friend, Asma. I'd really like to invite her.' So, in the end, Asma agreed.

Kate was really excited.

'What's it going to be like?' she said. 'What do I have to wear?'

'Oh, just dress to impress,' I said. 'It's the last part of the wedding. A big party. But don't wear anything too skimpy.'

'What, not too much bare flesh and cleavage?'

I laughed. 'You've got it!'

Kate was gobsmacked by the whole thing. To my relief she behaved really well and even Ammi remarked on how much she had changed, how 'modest' she had become. I knew it was all an act, but I was grateful to Kate for trying.

'It was fantastic, Halima,' she said later. 'Brilliant! I've never been to anything like it. All that colour – and those jewels!'

'A wedding's a really big deal for us,' I said.

'Hey,' said Kate. 'There were some fit-looking blokes there, too. I saw all your aunties and cousins sizing them up.'

I laughed. 'That's all part of it. Weddings are great places to meet a husband or a wife. And the aunties never stop scheming and matchmaking!'

'Did you see anyone there you fancied?'

'If I had, I wouldn't tell you!'

'That's a yes, then?'

But I refused to be drawn.

Actually, I had met someone I really liked. He was a cousin of Habib's called Mahmood and, like Habib, he'd lived in London all his life. He was interesting and intelligent and I loved talking to him. I knew that the aunties and cousins were watching us, but I didn't care. I was so happy for Asma and pleased that our family was linked with Habib's family. Asma was lucky in her in-laws and lucky in her husband. I was sure that their marriage would work.

After all the excitement had died down and Asma and Habib were settled in their flat, I spoke to Ammi about Mahmood, the boy I'd met.

'He's a cousin of Habib's,' I said. 'He's a really nice boy.'

'Oh yes,' said Ammi, but there was no enthusiasm in her voice. I was puzzled. Was this my *ammi*, whose most cherished dream was to have her children well married?

'Perhaps he might do for me?' I said. I was only joking – but she turned on me.

'No!' she said harshly.

'Why not! Aren't I good enough for Habib's family?' I said angrily.

'You concentrate on your studies, Halima,' said Ammi. 'Baba's too busy looking for a girl for Khalil to think of you.'

I was astonished. Ever since Asma had been a teenager, there had been talk about who she would marry, yet here was Ammi telling me not to think of marriage for myself.

I shrugged it off. I was doing my A levels in the summer and I wanted to get a place at college. I wanted to study politics and economics at university and, although I never let on to my family, I still had a dream of one day going into politics.

So I had plenty to think about and I certainly didn't want to get married just yet. I supposed that Baba wanted to see Khalil settled before he thought of my future, and I was quite happy with that.

A few months later, the search began in earnest for a bride for Khalil.

I told Kate all about it.

'So, this will be another London wedding, will it?'

I shook my head. 'No. I don't think so. There's talk of going back to Pakistan for this one.'

'Have they found a girl for him, then?'

'Hmm. Sort of. Baba's got someone in mind, but...'

'But?'

I knew that Khalil had been seeing someone. He was very keen on the girl but, in Baba's eyes, she was quite unsuitable. She wasn't from our tribe, she wasn't a devout Muslim and she wasn't even Pakistani.

Khalil had tried to persuade Baba to accept her, but Baba would have nothing of it.

The rows they had reminded me of the dreadful time with Imran. But there was one big difference. Khalil couldn't stand up to Baba.

One night, Khalil and I were alone in the house, watching television in the front room. Neither of us was interested in the programme so I turned it off.

'Do you love this girlfriend of yours, Khalil?' I asked.

He made a face and looked down at his hands. 'Yeah. I guess.'

'And you want to marry her?'

'Well. Yes. But I can't, can I?'

'Baba might give in, if you keep on at him.'

He shrugged. 'He'll never budge. You know that.'

I frowned. 'But surely, if you really love her, you should fight for her, go against Baba.'

Khalil gave a mirthless laugh. 'And be turned out like Imran? No thanks.'

'So you'll leave this poor girl and marry whoever Baba finds for you?'

He said nothing, just picked at his teeth.

I stood up, suddenly sickened by his cowardice, and walked away. When I reached the door I turned back.

'And what about the girl Baba finds for you, Khalil? What sort of life will it be for her if you don't love her? Have you thought of that?'

'I'll be kind to her. She'll do OK.'

'Huh!'

Kind. She'll do OK. What sort of basis for marriage is that? I thought. But maybe it was better than many Pakistani women could expect.

When I told all this to Kate, she raised her eyebrows. 'Ah, so it's not always ideal, then, this arranged marriage business.'

'Oh. It probably works OK most of the time. I still think it's better than your system.'

Kate blushed and turned away.

I had said the words without thinking. The moment

they slipped out, I regretted them. I had forgotten that Kate's parents were divorcing.

'Kate, I'm so sorry.'

She swallowed. 'No, our system's not perfect, that's for sure, but at least my parents *can* split up. Honestly, Halima, they'll will be much happier living apart – and I won't have to listen to their rows.'

I thought about Ammi then. Was she happy? Kate read my thoughts.

'It's different for your mum. She'd never leave your dad, would she, even if she was really unhappy?'

I shook my head. 'No. She'd never leave him – and she'll always give in to him. She was only a child when she married. I don't suppose she expected much from her marriage except children and security. She accepts what life has given her. I don't suppose she thinks much about being happy.'

'But you, Halima, you have expectations, don't you?'

I laughed and punched her on the arm. 'You know I have! I want it all. I want a good man who respects me, a terrific job and children, too, one day.'

'Huh!' said Kate, 'I've gone off the whole idea of marriage. I'm just going to have a string of lovers and a fantastic career.'

CHAPTER TWELVE

Much to Baba's excitement, I was accepted at City University to study International Politics. It was quite a long journey in on the Underground, but it did mean I could still live at home, which is what he wanted.

I was certainly ready to leave school, but there were people I would miss – Kate, of course, more than anyone. My brilliant, wild Kate had got into Oxford. Our school was so proud of her – only a handful of their students had ever got into Oxbridge and her photo was splashed all over the local paper – but I knew it would suit her. There she would be challenged in the way she loved challenging others. And she would thrive.

The other person I would miss was Miss Brunner. Those sessions at her debating club had opened my mind so much to other points of view, other ways of life. Before I left, I went to see her.

She hugged me. 'Well, Halima, this course you've chosen should suit you really well. I'll expect to see you in Parliament one day! Now, you be sure to make something of your life, won't you? You've got a good brain and an enquiring mind. Don't waste them.'

I smiled. 'I'll do my best, but ...'

She frowned. 'But what?'

I sighed. 'My dad will expect me to marry as soon as I leave college.'

'So?'

'Well, you know how it is with us.' I hesitated. 'It could be a struggle to have a career.'

'But surely, if you have an understanding husband?'

'Mm,' I said, uncertainly. That was a big *if*. I would probably have to fight for my independence. But maybe, if Habib's cousin... now there was someone who understood – and surely Baba would approve of him?

I thought of Asma. She was so lucky. She and Habib were happy together and he was a good, intelligent man. She was pregnant now and they were thrilled – and of course Baba and Ammi were over the moon. Asma seemed quite content to be a housewife and she hadn't worked since leaving college. But I was different. I wanted a career. Somehow I would find my way into politics.

Miss Brunner put her hand on my arm. 'Well, if you ever want to talk to someone about your future, you be sure to come and see me, won't you?'

'Thanks,' I said.

I started at college in the autumn. It was where Asma had been and there were a lot of Muslim girls there, so I felt comfortable. Some had come from our school so I already had a nucleus of friends, but other Muslim schoolfriends had not been allowed to go on to college and had already been married off.

Work was going well. I didn't find it easy but I really enjoyed the stimulus and buzz of college life – and my debating skills grew as they were challenged all the time.

At home, Ammi had bought the most beautiful red chiffon for my wedding *dupatta* as well as loads of sequins, beads and cut glass. But I had no time for embroidery.

'Halima, you'll never finish your *dupatta!*' cried Ammi.

I laughed. 'I'll finish it in time for my wedding, Ammi, I promise.'

And to please her, I did make a start on it.

Asma and Habib lived quite close to the nearest Underground to our house and sometimes I called in on my way home. Asma was eight months pregnant and wrapped up in preparing for the baby. The flat was full of baby clothes and equipment and the spare room had been turned into a nursery.

I didn't often see Habib because he was usually

still at work when I called, but one day I was much later than usual, and he was there.

And so was his cousin – Mahmood – the man I'd met at their wedding. It was so unexpected, that at first I found myself blushing and stammering when we were reintroduced, but soon we were chatting naturally, just as we'd done at the wedding.

Instead of sidelining me, as usually happened when there were two Pakistani men in the room, Mahmood made a point of talking to me. We chatted about all the people at the wedding and I giggled at his description of one particularly oily fellow with a deformed little finger.

'Who was that guy, anyway?' Mahmood asked Habib.

Habib shrugged. 'No idea. Not one of our side.'

'Oh, I know who you mean,' said Asma. 'He's a really distant cousin who was asking Baba to help him get a visa, and Baba was in such a good mood, he invited him along to the wedding.'

Asma went through to the kitchen and Mahmood and I went on talking. He asked all about my course at college and my career plans and I found myself confiding to him that I wanted to go into politics.

Time flew by, and suddenly I realised that Mahmood had been asked to dinner.

I got up, embarrassed. 'I must go home. They'll

be expecting me.'

'Why don't you stay?' said Habib. 'Ring your parents and tell them you're eating with us.'

I didn't need any persuading. And anyway, it wasn't that unusual for me to eat with them, so Ammi was quite happy when I phoned.

'Ask Habib to walk home with you, Halima. You hear me? You're not to come home on your own in the dark.'

'Habib, will you walk home with me after dinner?'

He grinned. 'Of course, little sister.'

It was one of the happiest evenings of my life. Mahmood had travelled a lot and he knew so much about other countries. And he asked for my opinions and listened to them, sometimes agreeing and sometimes not. He treated me as an equal. I'd never met a man from my own background whom I found so interesting or attractive.

He wasn't particularly good-looking, but he was so alive – and so funny. My sides ached with laughing as he teased me or told us silly stories about his family or his job.

When finally Habib and I set off for my home, I couldn't wipe the grin off my face.

'You like Mahmood, don't you, Halima?'

I looked down at my feet. It wouldn't do to be too enthusiastic. 'Yes, I like him very much.

He's an interesting man.'

'He's my favourite cousin,' said Habib.

And that was all that was said. But I knew that Asma would tell Ammi and Baba that she had introduced me to a suitable young man. And I couldn't believe that Baba or Ammi would disapprove of him. I knew he wasn't married, though there was always the possibility that his family might have someone else in mind for him. But somehow, I didn't think so. He was so obviously his own man and I guessed that, although he was looking for a Pakistani girl, for sure, he definitely wanted a girl with a mind of her own.

I held my breath, waiting for a reaction from my parents. However, the days passed and nothing happened. I was puzzled. I was so sure that Asma would have told them.

Then I was invited to dinner with Asma again.

I was really excited. Maybe they would invite Mahmood too! I dressed with extra care and arrived at the door of their flat nervous and excited.

But when I went inside, Asma was on her own.

'Where's Habib?'

Asma didn't meet my eyes. 'Oh, he's out tonight,' she said. 'Don't worry. He'll be back in time to walk you home.'

I hid my disappointment and we chatted on about her pregnancy and the names they had chosen for the baby. Once or twice I tried to talk about Mahmood, but she always changed the subject.

She was tense. I could sense it, and, after we had eaten, I said gently. 'Is everything OK, Asma?'

She put out her hand and led me over to the sofa. We sat side by side.

'I have some wonderful news for you, Halima.'

I was so excited, I couldn't help myself. I blurted it out: 'Mahmood?'

She looked startled. 'What? No. Nothing to do with Mahmood.'

'Oh.'

'No Halima. This is about your future.'

I must have looked puzzled.

'Silly girl. Your marriage!'

'My marriage,' I repeated, stupidly. 'What do you mean?'

'I mean that Baba has found you a husband!' She hugged me. 'Isn't that exciting?'

I stared at her. Nothing to do with Mahmood. That meant Baba had someone else in mind.

'But I thought you'd told him about Mahmood,' I stuttered.

She studied her hands. 'Yes, yes I did. He's a lovely man, Halima, and if Baba hadn't already...'

'What! You mean Baba's already approached someone?'

She nodded.

'When? He's never said anything to me.'

'Well, no. Nor to me. But apparently it was all arranged a long time ago. Back in Pakistan.'

There was a tight knot of dread in my stomach. 'How? What do you mean?'

Poor Asma. I knew she was finding it difficult. She was torn between loyalty to Baba and loyalty to me. But all I could see was Mahmood's laughing eyes, and I felt sick with anger.

'Do you remember when there was all that trouble about Baba's land?'

I nodded. 'Vaguely.'

Asma licked her lips, then continued. 'Well, the cousin who helped him out, who solved the problem for him…'

Suddenly, I knew exactly what had happened. I was back in the village again, eight years old, running home from school and seeing Baba at the well talking to a man I didn't recognise, and Baba was calling me over and introducing me to the man as a good and obedient child.

My heart was thumping against my ribs. 'He promised me to that man?'

Asma shook her head. 'No, no, not the old man. But he promised you to his son.'

I leapt up from the sofa. The sobs were rising

from my chest. I couldn't stop them.

'My God, Asma! I can't believe it. How could he?'

'Calm down, Halima. You know nothing about the son. Baba says he's got a marvellous job. He works in Saudi Arabia. It will be a good match.'

'How can you say that?' I spat at her. 'It's OK for you. You were lucky. You've got a lovely husband. And now, just as I meet someone... My God, Asma, why didn't Baba promise *you* to this man's son? You were the older one.'

She shrugged. 'Just luck, I guess...' she said, 'that you happened to be there at that moment.'

I started crying in earnest then. 'I can't do this. I won't.'

'Don't be stupid, Halima. You know what will happen if you refuse. It's a matter of honour. Baba promised you, and he won't break that promise.'

I couldn't speak any more. I was crying too much.

'Look. They'll let you speak to the boy on the phone. Don't do anything stupid. Think of the consequences.'

I blew my nose and looked at her miserably. She didn't need to spell it out. I thought of Imran. How much worse would it be for me if I went against Baba's wishes?

When Habib walked me home that night, I thought back to the journey we'd made together only a few short evenings ago. How happy I had been then, walking on air. I was sure, then, that Habib was pleased I liked his cousin – but that was before he and Asma were told about Baba's deal. And now, walking by his side, I was weighed down, my feet leaden and my spirits lower than they had ever been.

Habib squeezed my arm when he delivered me back to our house. 'Don't do anything to annoy your parents, Halima,' he said.

I didn't reply. I saw it all. I was the bait which had sealed the deal all those years ago.

And now it was payback time.

CHAPTER THIRTEEN

At home, I challenged Ammi.

'Why didn't you tell me this before? Why did you keep it from me?'

Ammi sighed. 'What for? Nothing will happen until you finish your studies. It is a good match for you, Halima. You should be pleased.'

Baba was furious when I said I didn't want to marry this unknown man.

'Ungrateful girl!' he yelled at me. 'He is from a good family, making a lot of money in Saudi. Of course you will marry him.'

'The wife of a migrant worker in Saudi Arabia! What sort of life would I have there? How could you promise me to him, Baba? How could you?'

'Be quiet, Halima. How dare you insult me!'

'Dare!' I shouted back at him. 'You didn't even dare tell me about him. You left Asma to do your dirty work.'

Baba's eyes flashed and he raised his hand. I ducked out of his way and ran upstairs to my room, slamming the door behind me.

I phoned Kate. I had to speak to someone outside the family. To my amazement, she didn't immediately rail against my family, my religion and arranged marriages.

'Look, calm down, Halima.'

There was a noise at the other end of the line.

'Hang on a sec, I'll just get rid of this lot.'

I heard laughing, and with a pang I realised that she'd moved on, had another set of friends, maybe even another best friend. Suddenly I felt unbearably lonely.

Then she was back on the phone. 'OK. Let's think this through. Remember what you said about Asma's marriage and how good it is?'

'Yes, but...'

'Well, give this guy a chance. You've not met him, right?'

'No.'

'Or even spoken to him on the phone?'

'Well no, but...'

'How about you asking if you can speak to him? You never know, he might be great.'

I was silent. She went on.

'Halima. Remember what happened to Imran. You've explained to me so many times how it is in your family. If, when you meet the guy, you can't stand him, then fair enough, you can refuse to marry him. But just think what will happen if you do. It won't be easy, will it?'

'I know, Kate. I know, you don't have to tell me that. But…' I took a deep breath.

'There's someone else,' I whispered, afraid that if I spoke normally, someone in the house might hear me.

'What?'

'I've met someone I really like and he's the right background and everything. If it wasn't for this stupid deal that Baba did, my parents would be sure to approve of him.'

'Ah. That does change things. Does he like you?'

'We've only met twice, but yes, yes – I'm sure he does.'

'Hmm.'

'What shall I do, Kate?'

'You're asking me! Hey, I'm only a non-believing Irish girl. What do I know?'

I laughed, in spite of myself.

'That's better. Now listen, I'm coming up to see you.'

'Oh Kate, that'd be great. When?'

'On Tuesday. I don't have any lectures then. I'll get the Oxford Tube up to town and meet you at your college.'

'You're a star!'

'I know I am. Meanwhile, my little friend, don't do anything stupid. Let's talk this through when we meet.'

The next morning, I went downstairs feeling calmer. Despite all the teasing about my way of life, Kate did understand. And she was clear-thinking. I wouldn't say any more against this boy until I'd spoken to her.

But Baba had other ideas.

The next evening, when I came in from college, he was standing in the hall chatting on the phone, beaming with pleasure. He beckoned me over.

'Here she is,' he said into the phone. Then he handed it over to me. 'Here, Halima. This is the young man I told you about. He would like to speak to you.'

I had no time to prepare myself. I picked up the phone. Think of Kate, I told myself. Don't rock the boat.

'Hello,' I said, my voice flat.

He had a deep voice. It was not unpleasant. I let him talk – about himself, about his job, about his prospects and how he'd always known that his father had helped my father. He mentioned this several times: how his father had rescued mine from a difficult situation.

I answered politely. A good and obedient child. That was how Baba had described me to this man's father all those years ago.

I played the part. I asked the right questions and when, at last, I put the phone down, Baba was rubbing his hands together.

'Good girl. You were very polite. What did he say?'

'Oh, he just told me about himself,' I said. 'And he'll phone again.'

'Excellent. You'll get to know each other.'

I nodded. But my resolve was hardening. The man had not asked a single question about me, about my studies, my interests, my ambitions. To me, he was typical of so many.

And this man was not Mahmood…

I did a lot of thinking in the next few days, before meeting up with Kate. If I refused to consider this man as a husband, there would be trouble. I spoke to Asma, who told me not to go against Baba. Then I spoke to Imran on the phone, thinking that he'd be sympathetic, but he didn't encourage me to say no, either.

'Wait until you get to know him, Halima. Talk to him some more on the phone. He sounds a good prospect.'

'A good prospect,' I said bitterly. 'Is that it?'

Imran sighed. 'Look, little sister, if you dig your toes in and refuse to marry him, you know what will happen?'

'I know.'

'Then don't do it. I tell you, you don't want to be cut off, like me. It's not a lot of fun.'

I didn't tell him about Mahmood, and changed the subject. 'How's the job?'

I could almost see him shrugging on the other end of the phone. 'It's a job. It pays the rent.'

And are you seeing any of your old friends?'

'Yeah.' He hesitated and then gave a harsh laugh. 'You soon find out who your real friends are.'

'But... you're not unhappy?'

There was a long silence. 'I'm glad to be away from Baba – but it's not easy being away from the family,' he said at last. 'Think very hard before you put yourself in my position, little sister. It would be much, much worse for you.'

'I know,' I said quietly.

Was I strong enough to resist my family? Was I right to resist? If I'd never met Mahmood, I might have gone along with the arrangement. The trouble was, I didn't know what Mahmood felt for me. Even if he did have the feelings I hoped he had, would he support me if I was condemned by my family? He would have to be very strong to do that.

If only I'd known him longer, if only I knew him better. Every instinct told me that he was the right man for me, but how could I be sure after only two meetings? My head told me I was being stupid and impetuous, that I should toe the line and not stir up trouble. My heart told me something else.

These thoughts went round and round in my brain as I tossed and turned in bed at night. I longed to see Kate and talk it through with her. I was counting the hours until the following Tuesday.

And then the guy from Saudi phoned again.

Baba spoke to him first, before handing the phone over to me. This time I listened to his voice really carefully, trying to picture the man behind it. I tried to ask him some probing questions but he cut me short with a laugh, as though I was a silly child. The more he went on – about his lifestyle in Saudi Arabia, his flat, his car – the more sure I was that I could not live with him.

And then he said something which made me absolutely certain.

'It's good that your family is honouring their debt,' he said. 'You are owed me.'

And although he said it with a laugh, my whole body tensed.

'You are owed me' – as if I was a consignment of goods already paid for.

I had no doubts now. I could never possibly spend the rest of my life with a man who thought like that.

Somehow I ended the conversation without losing my temper.

Baba stroked my cheek. 'Good girl, good girl,' he said. 'And guess what, Halima?'

'What?'

'He's coming to Pakistan for Khalil's wedding. So you'll meet your future husband there. Isn't that exciting? You can have a *magni* there!'

I nodded, not trusting myself to speak. Khalil's wedding was only a couple of months away. We had met the girl Baba had chosen for him. She was nice enough, plain but pleasant, and she ticked all the right boxes. Khalil had been through the motions, asked her family and there had been a *magni*, but there was no spark between them. I knew that Khalil still loved his old girlfriend and I felt really sad for his bride-to-be.

However, once again the families had gone into action. Uncles and aunties here and in Pakistan were busy making preparations for the wedding. And it would be a huge one, with people coming from all over to be there.

Including the guy from Saudi.

If I went to Khalil's wedding in Pakistan, our families would announce our engagement to the world.

And if I met him, and told Baba I didn't want to marry him?

I shuddered. Unlike Asma's marriage, where she could have refused, this arrangement was different.

It was a matter of family honour and I had no choice. If I refused, my father would enforce the marriage – and I knew exactly how he would do that.

How I had despised those girls at school who had meekly gone off to Pakistan to be married. That would never happen to me, I'd thought. My family's not like that. They'd never force me to marry anyone.

CHAPTER FOURTEEN

Mahmood

I've never met a girl like Halima.

As soon as I saw her, at Habib's wedding, I knew she was different. She intrigued me with her quirky smile and her big eyes flashing with anger as she talked about something that had upset her. She didn't set out to impress me, not like some of the others. She was just herself: bright, interested – and attractive.

She even laughed at my jokes!

She has plans, too. She wants a good career. She can see beyond all the plotting and matchmaking that goes on amongst the older women. There's so much more to her than dressing up and flirting to snare some boy into marriage. She's got a good mind and she could do so much. She'll go far.

If she's allowed to.

It was great that we met up again at Habib's place. It was the best evening! We talked and talked – and laughed. I felt we'd never run out of things to say to one another.

I rang Habib the next day. 'I really like your sister-in-law,' I said. And he'd laughed. 'I think she likes you, too, cousin.'

But the next time I saw Habib, he told me to put her out of my mind.

'Her dad's set up a marriage for her,' he said.

I hadn't expected to feel so angry and upset. After all, I'd only met her twice.

'And she's agreed?' I asked. I couldn't believe that Halima would meekly cave in. Especially after the way she'd been with me. She was so open and excited about her course and her future.

'Well, put it like this,' said Habib. 'She hasn't said no.'

'So, what's the deal. Who is this guy?'

And then Habib explained.

I could see it all. *Family honour.* Is there anything more deadly? But poor girl, what can she do? If she refuses to marry the man, she'll probably be forced into it anyway. I know how fathers can manipulate their daughters.

God, what a mess.

And I can't do anything to help her. I have no claim on her. I'm good friends with her sister, and she's told me to keep my nose out of her family's business.

For all I know, she may not object to this marriage. Asma's right. It is nothing to do with me, but I wish

I knew if it is what Halima wants.

And I wish I could put those laughing eyes out of my mind. And the way her face turns from solemn to mischievous when she smiles.

CHAPTER FIFTEEN

Halima

Tuesday at last! Kate and I met in the college canteen. Impetuous as ever, she rushed over and hugged me. Then she held me away from her.

'You look terrible!'

I smiled. 'Thanks!'

'Sorry, but you do. You look so sad – and pale.'

'I've not been sleeping much.'

Kate pushed me back on to my seat. 'Stay there, I'll get some tea.'

I watched her as she wove her way in and out of the tables, carrying a tray back to me. Just by the way she moved, by the confidence of her smile, I could tell that her horizons were expanding, that she was relishing her new life. She put the tray down and sat opposite me.

'Oxford suits you,' I said, smiling.

She picked up her cup of tea and sipped thoughtfully.

'Yeah! It does. I love it. But we're here to talk

about you. Tell me all about it.'

I had chosen a spot tucked away from prying eyes so that we could speak privately. As I told her all that had happened in the last few weeks, I started to cry.

Kate put her hand across the table and held mine.

'Halima,' she said softly, 'you can't give in to this. You know you can't.'

When at last I could speak again, I whispered, 'I'm so tired, Kate. I've been over and over it and I can't see a way out, unless I leave home and break with my family.'

Kate eyes held mine. 'Then you may have to.'

'But I don't want to. What would I do? I'd have to quit college. They wouldn't pay for me any more. I'd lose all my friends and relations.'

Kate was still holding my hand. She gave it a tight squeeze.

'Not all of them,' she said firmly. 'Not the ones who matter.'

I gave her a weak smile. 'I'd lose my sister,' I said.

'Asma! Surely not.'

I nodded. 'If I went against Baba, she wouldn't be strong enough to keep seeing me. She's told me as much.'

'No!'

I nodded. 'She's said that it's different now she's married and expecting a baby. If she takes my side in all this, then she'll be shunned, too. I can understand it. She needs the family's help. And even Imran told me not to go against Baba.'

Kate gently withdrew her hand. She leant back in her chair and locked her hands behind her head.

'When are all the family going to Pakistan for Khalil's wedding?' she asked.

I found a tissue and wiped my nose. 'Just as soon as Asma's had the baby. Ammi wants to make sure everything's OK before the rest of the family leave.'

'So Asma and Habib are staying here?'

I nodded. 'Yes. They don't want to travel with a new baby.'

'Mm,' said Kate thoughtfully. 'So you've only got a few weeks to make your own plans.'

'I've no idea what to do, Kate. I can't bear the thought of marrying this guy, but if I go to Pakistan for the wedding, my father will force me to.'

'Don't be stupid, Halima. He can't! There's a law against forced marriage now. Your father could be prosecuted.'

I looked at her sadly. 'There's a law in *this* country. But someone would have to report him, and who would do that? Can you imagine what would happen if *I* did that? No one in my family would ever speak to me again.'

She frowned, and I went on, speaking slowly

and clearly. 'My father has my passport and if I go to Pakistan, he'll make sure I can't get my hands on it. I'll probably be kept a virtual prisoner until I agree to marry the guy, and if I still refuse, I'll be at Baba's mercy. I won't be able to leave and he – and the rest of the family – will put all sorts of pressure on me. Not only them, but all the cousins and aunties and uncles in my village – and the elders too, probably. I'll be seen as bringing shame on my family and I'll be disowned. No other Pushtoon boy will want me then, and my father certainly won't allow me back to England to finish college. It's a lose-lose situation.'

Kate looked horrified. 'But… I thought your family were different. You always told me your father would never force you to marry anyone.'

'That's what I thought, Kate. But this is different. It's a matter of honour. My father promised me to this guy all those years ago. He promised me in payment for a favour done for him. And my father won't break his word.'

'I see,' said Kate, quietly, her voice flat and cold. 'He won't break his word. He'll just break his daughter.'

I nodded.

'Jesus Christ, Halima, this is medieval! How can your precious religion condone this?'

I smiled. 'I thought you didn't believe in him.'

'Who?'

'Jesus Christ.'

Kate laughed. 'I don't. I just need to call out to some god or other. The circumstances demand it.'

I laughed. It was the first time in ages. 'Hey, it's really good to see you.' I paused. 'And by the way, before you go rubbishing my religion, Islam's got nothing to do with forced marriage. There's nothing about it in the Koran. It's just a notion dreamt up by control-freak men.'

'OK, OK. Point taken.' Then she looked at me long and hard. I could practically see the cogs grinding in her brain.

'Right,' she said at last. 'This is what we do.'

'We?'

'I'm not leaving here until you've made some plans,' she said firmly.

'But…'

'No buts. Finish your tea and dry your eyes. We're going to see Miss Brunner.'

'Miss Brunner?'

'Stop repeating everything I say. Come on. If we hurry we can get to the school before she leaves for home.'

'But I've got a lecture...'

'Oh, for goodness sake, Halima, forget the lecture. This is your future we're talking about here. If we don't get something sorted out, there'll be no more lectures – and no more college.'

She dragged her phone out of her pocket.

'What are you doing?'

'What does it look like? I'm phoning the school. Leaving a message for Miss Brunner.'

'Hang on,' I said. 'I've got her mobile number.'

Kate frowned. 'How come?'

'She said to contact her if I wanted to talk about my future.'

'Well,' said Kate. 'There you go. Phone her now.'

Miss Brunner's mobile kicked into voicemail and I left a message. I didn't really know what to say, so in the end I just said I needed to speak to her urgently and that Kate and I were on our way to the school.

Miss Brunner phoned back while we were on the bus. She sounded a bit harassed.

'Halima. Is this really urgent? Can it wait? I've got a staff meeting after school.'

My hands were sweaty against the phone. 'Well, I suppose...'

Kate grabbed the phone from me. 'Please see us. We're almost there, Miss Brunner. It won't take long and it is really urgent.'

Miss Brunner was talking and Kate nodded. 'Yes. Well I can't tell you much on the phone but it's about a forced marriage.'

She nodded again. 'Yes. Halima.'

More talking, then Kate said goodbye. She punched the air. 'Yes! She'll see us as soon as we get there.'

It was strange going back to the school. I'd not been there since the day I left. As we got off the bus outside the gates I watched the pupils streaming out into the road chatting, shouting, laughing. I spotted Miss Brunner standing talking to a group of girls. She looked up and smiled as we approached.

The girls drifted off and she took us inside.

'We'll use your old classroom,' she said. 'There's no one there. We can talk freely.'

Kate and I automatically sat down at desks and Miss Brunner sat on the teacher's table, one leg swinging lazily. I looked at her with new eyes. She was young – only a few years older than us, and yet, when I'd been her pupil, she had seemed much older.

I glanced round the classroom. It had only been a few months, but everything had changed. The notices on the wall were different, the walls were newly painted.

'Now,' said Miss Brunner, 'What's this all about?'

As clearly as I could, I tried to explain the situation. Every now and then, Kate interrupted with some acerbic comment.

'Hush, Kate,' said Miss Brunner. 'You're not helping.'

'Sorry, Miss.'

I went on with my story, I held nothing back. I told her about Imran and I even told her about Mahmood – and I told her how I couldn't report my father because of what it would do to the family. When I'd finished, there was a long silence. The only noises were our collective breathing and Miss Brunner's fingers drumming on the table-top.

Kate couldn't bear the suspense. 'Well, can you help her, Miss?' she blurted out.

Miss Brunner raised her head. 'I want to help you, Halima – I'm just trying to think how.'

I nodded. 'I don't want to put any pressure on you, Miss,' I said. 'It could be dangerous.'

Miss Brunner was no fool. She knew I wasn't being over-dramatic. She'd been teaching Pakistani girls long enough to know that there could be a price to pay for interfering in family matters.

'I know,' she said quietly. 'That's why I have to think about it very carefully.'

Another silence, then she stood up and started walking up and down. She stopped, and turned to me. 'What is it you want to do, Halima? Ideally?'

I cleared my throat. 'I want to finish college and get a good job.'

'And you say that if you refuse to marry this man, your family won't pay your college fees?'

'Not only that. They'll have nothing more to do with me.'

'Are you sure?'

I thought of Imran. 'Quite sure,' I said.

'And you say that if you go to Pakistan for your brother's wedding, you'll not be allowed to return unless you agree to marry this man. Has your father actually said that?'

I shook my head.

'Not in so many words, no. But I know him. And it's about family honour, Miss. If I go, he'll make me marry the man.'

She took a deep breath. 'Then you must not go.'

'But how can I...?'

'I think you have to be very brave, Halima. If you really don't want this marriage, then you must leave home.'

I felt numb.

'You are quite sure you don't want the marriage?'

I licked my dry lips. 'This man thinks of me as some sort of asset. A trophy, like his car or his apartment in Riyadh. I've spoken to him several times on the phone. He told me I was owed to him. After all you've taught me, after all I've learnt here, I can't live with a man who thinks like that.' I paused. 'And my life in Saudi would be really restricted. I'd not be allowed out on my own. I'd have no freedom. And, whatever my father says, the guy is just a migrant worker. He may be earning good money, but I would have no status as his wife.'

'Right. As long as you are absolutely sure.'

I nodded.

'Then you have to leave here.'

'What – leave Walthamstow?'

She came over to me then, and cupped my chin in her hand. 'I don't think you have a choice, Halima. From what you've told me, there is no alternative. You'll have to get right away from here, from your family, from your friends.'

'But where can I go?' I could feel tears coming.

Kate stretched over and squeezed my hand.

Miss Brunner frowned. 'If you leave it with me, I can probably help you to get into another college where they do much the same course as you're doing now.'

'But how would I pay the fees?'

Miss Brunner started to pace up and down again. 'In cases like yours – exceptional cases – the local authority might agree to pay for you. I'll see what I can do.'

'But where is the college?'

'The one I have in mind isn't that far away, but it's outside London.'

'And how would I live?'

Kate interrupted. 'Give her a chance, Halima! She can't think of everything at once!'

'Sorry. I'm so sorry, Miss.' I was crying now.

Miss Brunner smiled. 'Look, I'll see what I can arrange and I'll get back to you. Meanwhile, just act as if you are happy to go off to Pakistan for the wedding, and wait until I contact you.'

'But we leave quite soon. The baby's due any moment, and we'll go as soon as term's finished.'

'I'll start making enquiries right away. Trust me, Halima.'

'Thanks so much,' said Kate. 'You don't know how much it means to her.'

'Oh yes, I think I do,' Miss Brunner said quietly, 'otherwise I wouldn't get involved.' Then she looked at her watch. 'Now I must go to this meeting. I'm already late.'

She picked up her bag. 'Come on. I'll see you out.'

We said goodbye and she walked away, but suddenly she stopped and came running back. 'Halima,' she said. 'You will make sure you delete any calls you receive from me, won't you?'

And it was then that the enormity of what I was doing, of what I was asking her to do, hit home. My stomach clenched tight. This wasn't just dangerous for me, it was dangerous for her, too.

I nodded. 'Of course. I'll be really careful.'

CHAPTER SIXTEEN

It was such a strain trying to act normally. Ammi started worrying about me.

'You look so pale, Halima, and you're not eating properly. What's the matter with you?'

How I longed to tell her. My poor Ammi! I was going to break her heart.

'I'm nervous,' I said. This was absolutely true. I was desperately nervous about what I had started. But there was no going back.

'Why? About meeting your new husband?'

'Of course.'

Ammi hugged me. 'Oh, he's so right for you, Halima. Good family, good job. He will make you very happy. For sure, he will make you very happy. You are a lucky girl.'

I kept to my room when I was at home, saying I had to study, but most of the time I lay on my bed staring at the ceiling, waiting for Miss Brunner to phone. The rest of the time I sorted out the things I needed to take with me. A few clothes, books, important papers – and my embroidery silks and needles. I would have to live without my passport. Baba had that, and it was locked away in a drawer in their bedroom. And I'd take a photo of Asma and Habib's wedding. It had all my family in it – all except Imran, of course – and in the background there was another face: Mahmood's. Whenever my resolve weakened, I would pick up the photo and stare into his laughing eyes to give myself the strength not to cave in. I'd probably never see him again, but at least he'd shown me that there were Muslim men like him in the world, men who would treat me as an equal. Men who would not say such things as, 'You are owed me'.

Asma was overdue now. She asked me over to keep her company and we went for a walk in the local park.

'So, you've agreed to marry the boy from Saudi?' she said.

Her remark caught me unawares. 'I don't know,' I stuttered. 'I want to meet him first.'

She took my arm. 'I'm so glad you're not making a big fuss about it,' she said.

I shrugged. 'What else can I do?'

She nodded. 'I know, it's difficult for you. It's a pity Baba made that promise, but he'll never go back on his word. And the guy does sound a good match for you.'

We had come to a bench and she sank down on it, breathless and heavy. She turned to me and took my hands in hers. 'You will agree to marry him, won't you. You won't make trouble for the family?'

Trouble for the family. Always the family. What about me – what about *my* feelings?

I bit back my response, and shrugged. 'I want to meet him first,' I said firmly.

She knew only too well what would happen if I refused him and, in her own way, she was trying to warn me, tell me that refusing would do no good. It would only make it worse for me.

I hated deceiving her, but I knew she'd never keep my secret.

Luckily for me, the baby came the very next day so all the family's attention was focused on that. A beautiful baby boy.

Ammi was on the phone all the time chatting to the aunties and recounting every detail of Asma's labour.

I didn't go to see the baby in hospital but Ammi and Baba did, and when they came back they were over the moon with excitement.

'Oh, such a perfect baby. Such a strong little boy. He looks just like Habib!'

I waited until Asma was back home before I went to see them. Luckily, there were no other relations around when I went, so I was able to have some time alone with Asma and Habib and the baby.

Asma handed him to me. I took him and smiled into his crinkled face. I put my finger into his little fist and he hung on to it.

'He's lovely,' I said. And I really meant it. But he didn't look like Habib. I thought he looked much more like Imran.

Then I started to cry. I was crying a lot at the moment. Anything would start me off.

'Don't cry, Halima,' said Asma. 'Just think. You'll have babies soon, once you're married.'

But I wasn't crying for the children I didn't have. I was crying because I knew that I might never get to know this little boy, my own nephew. Would Asma and Habib have anything to do with me after I'd left Walthamstow?

I wanted so much to talk to them about my plans, to make them understand.

☪☪☪

A few days later, Miss Brunner rang.

'Can you talk?'

'Yes,' I said. 'I'm on the bus. No problem.'

'OK. Listen carefully, Halima. Good news! I've got you a place at the college I told you about and I've been in touch with the local authorities. There are lots of papers to complete, but basically, they know your situation and they'll cover your fees.'

'Thank you. Thank you so much.' I suppose it was what I wanted but I could feel no enthusiasm, just an aching loneliness.

She sounded worried. 'Are you quite sure you want to do this, Halima?'

'Yes,' I said, trying to sound more positive. 'Yes, I'm quite sure. I have no choice.'

'Right. Well, the people at the college say you can go right away and live there during the vacation. There won't be any students about, of course, but there'll be people coming and going, and you'll be safe and have somewhere to stay.'

'So I can go there as soon as term ends here?'

'Yes,' she said. 'Is that OK?'

'That's such a relief, Miss. I'm really grateful.' Then reality kicked in. 'But I don't know how to get there. And there's all my things...'

'Don't worry, Halima, I've thought of that. If you can bring most of what you need to college, I'll collect you on the last day of term and drive you there.'

'But you're taking a big risk, Miss. What if someone sees you with me? Someone might tell my parents and my father would be so angry...'

'Yes,' she said. 'I've thought of that too.'

She had it all worked out and, in any other circumstances, the cloak and dagger stuff would have been quite funny. I was to get a cab from college to a road not far from her house. She'd be watching out for me and as soon as the cab had gone, she'd come and pick me up with all my belongings. Since she lived in an area where there were hardly any Pakistanis, it would be unlikely that any of my relations would see me.

The days dragged by. It was good that the rest of the family were so tied up with preparing for the trip to Pakistan, for Khalil's big wedding there and, of course, with the new baby. Ammi's feet hardly touched the ground. She was either on the phone chatting to the aunties, or rushing over to Asma's to check on the baby, or buying clothes and presents to take to Pakistan.

I was fitted for new clothes, too, clothes I knew I would never wear. I felt guilty that Baba was spending all this money on me – but what could I do?

'Turn round, Halima,' said Ammi, as I paraded in my new silks. She clapped her hands together. 'You look so pretty, darling, so slim now. Your new husband will be very pleased with you.'

I knew I had lost weight. The kilos had been dropping off. I couldn't face eating much because I was so worried.

'Look. Look in the mirror,' said Ammi.

I turned to the full-length mirror in the bedroom and looked at myself critically. How ironic that I was looking better, now, than I had ever looked. I tried to be enthusiastic.

'It's lovely, Ammi,' I said, and I gave her a tearful hug.

'Hey, don't cry, darling. You are going to be married.'

'Not just yet, Ammi,' I said. 'Baba said I could finish my studies before I get married.'

She shrugged. 'Of course, darling. Of course he did.'

She looked away from me and busied herself with the material of my outfit. I stared down at her. She was no good at keeping secrets. Was this guy from Saudi pressing for an early marriage? Surely he'd be satisfied with a *magni.* No honourable family would go back on a *magni.*

I started shaking. How much influence did the guy's family have over Baba? When he discovered I hadn't gone to Pakistan with my family, what would happen then? What excuses would Baba make?

'You're trembling, Halima. Whatever's the matter?'

'Nothing, Ammi, nothing. I'm just tired.'

'Too much studying,' said Ammi. 'It's not good

for you. Still, you'll soon be on holiday and in the sun again. Are you excited about going back home?'

Back home. Our village in Pakistan would always be home to her. I thought of it then with an acute longing – a longing which would never again be satisfied. Once I ran away, I'd never be able to go back there.

'Of course I'm excited,' I replied automatically. 'I can't wait to be there again.'

On the doormat, the next morning, I saw a letter from Saudi Arabia addressed to Baba. I skirted round it as I made my way out of the front door, as if, by touching it, I could become contaminated.

That evening, Baba waved the opened letter at me. 'A nice letter from the boy in Saudi, Halima – and look, he has sent a photo, too.'

Ammi came into the lounge, wiping her hands on a towel. 'He's a handsome fellow, isn't he, Halima? What a lucky girl you are.'

I took the photo from Baba and studied it closely. The guy wasn't bad-looking, but there was an arrogance about him which came through in the self-satisfied smirk and the cold eyes.

You are owed me. I could easily imagine him saying that. I handed the photo back.

'Yes, he's not bad-looking,' I said.

Every day I loaded up my backpack with more stuff

and took it to college. I had to be careful, so I was only taking absolute essentials. No one noticed. They were too busy with other things.

My safety valve was my phone. I only phoned Kate or Miss Brunner when I was out of the house, away from flapping ears.

I only spoke to Miss Brunner occasionally – just to reassure her that I was going ahead with my plans. And I met her once. She had come on a visit to my college with some of her students and, while they were being shown round, she met me in the canteen. Although it was quite natural that she should meet up with an old student, I felt very uneasy all the time we were together, but she had papers for me to sign and she had to go through them with me. I was even more nervous when one of the college tutors greeted her.

'Checking up on your old students?' he asked.

'Yes,' she said, smiling rather stiffly. 'I bumped into Halima in the corridor.'

When he walked away, she said, 'Once you've left here, you will write and tell the college what's going on, won't you?'

I looked shocked. 'I can't tell them where I am. My parents will be sure to contact them.'

'No. No need to tell them where you are. Just explain that you've transferred, explain your situation.'

How would I do that, I wondered, without giving it all away, without telling them where I'd gone, without mentioning Miss Brunner's involvement?

CHAPTER SEVENTEEN

It was the last day of term. The day I'd been dreading. I'd not slept at all, and I knew I looked pale and tired.

I woke early and went through my morning routine like a zombie. When I was ready to go down to breakfast, I stood at the door of my room looking in. Would I ever see it again? I tried to memorise everything: the bed, the cupboard, the faded carpet, the curtains at the windows. And in a corner of my bedroom, draped over a chair, my unfinished wedding *dupatta* with the boxes of threads and sequins and beads stacked on the seat of the chair. At the last moment, I stuffed the whole lot into my backpack, then I turned and closed the door softly behind me before heading downstairs.

I tried to spin out my breakfast, chewing everything several times, making my tea last longer than usual. And all the time I watched Ammi busying herself in the kitchen, her familiar figure scuttling hither and thither.

Stop! I wanted to shout. Stay still! Let me look at you! But when she did stop and speak to me, it was only to tell me to hurry up.

'No need to dawdle just because it's the last day of term,' she said. But she smiled at me as she spoke.

I held the smile in my memory. My darling Ammi. So proud of her student daughter and so concerned that I might be late on the last day of term. Poor Ammi. She would never feel proud of me again.

My heart ached fit to burst. I longed more than anything to put my arms round her and tell her that I loved her. That I didn't want to leave her. That none of this was her fault and that I understood why she had to support Baba.

But there was no way.

At last I could put it off my longer. I stood up and shrugged my backpack on.

'Bye, Ammi,' I said, trying to sound as natural as possible.

'Bye, darling.' She didn't even turn her head. 'See you later.'

See you later. But you won't, Ammi.

I hesitated at the door, and briefly she looked in my direction.

'Go on, Halima. Shoo! Whatever's the matter with you. Hurry up!'

Then she turned and walked towards the stairs.

I wanted so badly to run to her. I knew I had to walk out of the door as I did every morning, but my feet felt glued to the floor. Still I hesitated, looking down the passage to where she was standing calling up to Khalil to hurry, or he'd be late for work.

Tears began to well up. I couldn't bear it. I started moving back towards her for one last comforting hug. But then Khalil came crashing down the stairs and I came to my senses.

Idiot, I told myself. Act normally. I turned back and fumbled with the door handle, silent tears running down my cheeks. Once I was out of the house I started walking very fast up the street, sobbing loudly, great heaving, gasping sobs, past caring if anyone saw me.

It wasn't until I was on the Tube heading for college that I got myself under control. I felt completely drained, my limbs heavy and my brain fogged. I dragged myself through the day, going through the motions, telling myself that I mustn't think ahead. Just get through the next minute, the next hour. Eventually the day would end.

And so often, the image of Ammi came into my head. Busy, smiling, saying goodbye to me, just as she did every day. Getting on with her chores, chatting with the aunties, preparing food for us all. Home-making is all she knows, and her children are her life.

Ammi, I wish it could be different.

How hurt she would be when she knew what I had done.

The only people who knew about my plans were Kate and Miss Brunner – and staff at the new college. There were so many good friends whom I longed to tell. So many of them would understand why I was doing what I was doing, and would have wanted to give me support and advice. But it wasn't fair to involve them. It was better that they knew nothing, better that I cut myself off and disappeared from their lives.

All through that day I kept looking at my good friends, my fellow students, those I had laughed and chatted with, argued with, travelled with on the bus, sat beside as we studied. And all day, the talk seemed to be of what we were doing in our holidays.

'You're off to Pakistan, aren't you, Halima?'

'Yes. To my brother's wedding.'

'Hey. Will it be a big do?'

I nodded. 'Huge.' Quickly I directed the conversation back to them, to what their plans were. Would I ever see any of them again? I stared at each set of features in turn, trying to burn them into my memory.

The day ended at last, and then there was the problem of moving all my belongings. I had booked a taxi but I needed help with the bags and boxes.

Two of my friends heaved things outside for me.

'What's with all this stuff, Halima?'

I didn't know what to say, so I just shrugged and smiled. 'Oh, I don't know. I didn't realise I'd left so much here,' I said feebly.

At last, I was bundled into the taxi with all my belongings. My friends were still standing near me when I told the driver where to go, so I panicked and gave him my home address. Through the window I waved until the college was out of sight, and then I leaned forward and said I had changed my mind, and gave him the name of the street Miss Brunner had given me.

The driver screwed his head round and frowned, but I didn't offer any explanation.

Luckily, the cab driver wasn't anyone I recognised. One of my uncles drove a taxi, and it would have been just my luck if I'd got him as my driver.

It was a long journey, and I felt very nervous and sat rigidly upright, my fists clenched and my nails digging into the palms of my hands. My brain was frozen and I couldn't think straight, but I watched the route carefully, just in case the driver thought I was running away and decided to take me home. Stop being so paranoid! I told myself. But still, I was relieved when eventually we got there.

'What number?' asked the driver.

I cleared my throat. 'Twenty-nine.'

The cab crawled along the street checking the numbers.

'It has a red door,' I said helpfully. Miss Brunner had told me to get out there because it was easy to spot.

'OK. It's down there. I can see it now.'

He pulled up outside and helped me out with my luggage. He looked at it, piled up beside me on the pavement.

'Shall I help you inside with it, love?' he said, when I'd paid him.

I fought down my panic. 'No thanks. My uncle will be there. I've phoned him.'

Shut up! I thought to myself. There's no need to explain yourself to this man.

I watched as he drove off down the road. Was he looking in the mirror, waiting to see if I walked up to the door and rang the bell? I made a show of picking up some of my bags and then went slowly up the steps to the front door of number 29. When I reached the door I fiddled with my handbag, pretending to fish in it for keys, but all the time I was watching until the taxi reached the end of the street, turned right and was lost to view. Quickly I ran down the steps again and stood on the pavement.

What if Miss Brunner had decided not to come?

What if she didn't turn up? What if someone saw me and told my parents? What if…?

But almost immediately, Miss Brunner's car drew up beside me and I felt weak with relief.

She smiled as she jumped out of the car and came towards me. She gave me a quick hug, and then grabbed some of my bags and stuffed them in the car boot.

'Come on, Halima, don't stand there like a statue. Help me load this up. We want to get away from Walthamstow pronto.'

I was feeling unreal. I knew there was no going back, but I felt as if I was trapped in a dream. We heaved the last of the boxes of books into the back seat and then she jumped into the driving seat and I got in beside her.

We didn't speak much as she negotiated traffic and headed out of London to the motorway. Occasionally she glanced at me, smiled and asked if I was OK, and I nodded in return.

Gradually, as we drew further and further away from London, I began to relax, and once we hit the motorway, the worst of the tension began to drain away.

'I've hardly ever been out of Walthamstow,' I said. 'And I've never been in the country.'

Miss Brunner looked across at me. 'Everything's

going to be very different, Halima. The campus is not far from the nearest town but it's just a big country town. It's nothing like London.'

'Yes I know.'

When we'd been travelling for about an hour, Miss Brunner drove into a service station. We got out and stretched and then went into the café, sat down and had a drink and a sandwich.

'How are you feeling?'

I shook my head. 'I don't know. Excited. Confused. Guilty.'

She looked at me, her eyes serious. 'This is a huge step you're taking, Halima.' She hesitated. 'You might find yourself very lonely. There won't be any young people on the campus until the start of the academic year.'

I nodded. 'I know. But at least I'll be safe. And I'll have time to think.'

'What will you do about money?'

I was embarrassed. It was something that I'd been worrying about. 'I've got a bit that I saved from my weekend job in Walthamstow. That should tide me over for a while.'

'What did you do?'

'Oh, I worked in a shop helping out on Saturday mornings.'

'Well, maybe you can do something similar here –

at least in the vacations.'

'Yes,' I said uncertainly. 'I'll see if I can find something.'

Miss Brunner was still looking at me. 'You know,' she said slowly. 'It will be very different, don't you? There won't be as many Pakistani students around.'

I sighed. 'Yes, I realise that.'

There was an unspoken understanding that I would stand out. I wouldn't be able to blend into the crowd as I did in Walthamstow. If someone found out where I had gone, I would probably be easy to find.

Miss Brunner took a sip of coffee, then put down her cup and picked up a spoon. Absently, she stirred in some sugar.

'Halima, you don't think that your father will send someone to look for you, do you?'

I understood what she was driving at. There had been stories in the press about girls killed by their families because they refused to marry the man chosen for them. Honour killings.

My father had many faults, but he wouldn't want me harmed – I was quite certain of that. I shook my head.

'No. My family would never hurt me. As soon as I've settled in, I'll let them know I'm safe,' I said.

'And what will happen then? Won't they put pressure on you to come home?'

I shrugged. 'I'm not going to let them. I won't speak to them. I'll just send a text to Asma.'

'But surely they'll keep phoning your mobile?'

'I'll only answer if it's someone I want to speak to.'

I thought of Ammi and how worried she would be. Maybe I would speak to her, just once, just so she could hear my voice. No! I mustn't. I must be strong. I must cut off all contact, at least for now. That's the only way it would work.

Miss Brunner interrupted my thoughts. 'Will they still go to Pakistan for your brother's wedding?'

I laughed. 'Of course! There's no way they'd put that off. Imagine the shame!'

'What will they say about you? How will they explain that you're not with them?'

'Oh, they'll think of something,' I said bitterly. 'They'll stall. They'll make some excuse or other.'

I glanced at my watch. Would they be getting anxious yet? I was normally home from college by now. But perhaps they would think that I was late because it was the last day of term…

I would have to send a message soon.

We set off again and then, after a while, we turned off the motorway. I saw a sign to Oxford and pointed to it.

'I won't be too far from Kate,' I said.

Miss Brunner smiled. 'Yes, you can easily visit

each other. That'll be lovely for you.'

Well, it would be lovely once the new term began, but Kate was going to America for the vacation on some trip or other organised by the university. There were three long months before I would see her again. Three months to get through, on my own in a strange place with little or no company.

At last we were there. We drove through the gates and up a long tree-lined drive to the college buildings.

I had looked up the college online, so I shouldn't have been surprised – but it was so different, so leafy and green.

'It's beautiful!' I said. And I really meant it.

Miss Brunner looked relieved. 'I hope I made the right choice for you, Halima. I hope you'll be happy here.'

I suddenly felt overwhelmed by emotion. I couldn't reply.

I met the College Principal who had arranged for me to be transferred, and he introduced me to a couple of staff members.

'Do they all know about me?' I whispered to Miss Brunner, as we made our way up to the room where I was to stay.

'No. Just the Principal. You've not told anyone, have you?'

'No. Only Kate knows, and she won't say anything.'

We made several journeys up two flights of stairs and along a long corridor to my little room. There was a single bed, a built-in cupboard, some empty shelves along one wall, a desk under the window and an en-suite shower and toilet. I would be private and quiet.

Miss Brunner walked across to the window. 'Look, Halima, you can see right across the park. It's a beautiful view.'

I joined her at the window and stared out. The trees were in full leaf and the sun was shining. It was peaceful – a far cry from the noise and dirt of Walthamstow. I put my hand on her arm.

'Thank you,' I said. 'Thank you for bringing me here.'

She smiled at me, then she went and sat down on the bed. She had her serious face on.

'You will work hard, won't you?'

'Yes, I promise.'

'And Halima.' She hesitated.

'Yes?'

'You know that I can't do any more for you?'

'What do you mean?'

She looked uncomfortable. 'I've done this because I'm fond of you and I feel very strongly that you shouldn't be forced to marry against your will... and you're bright and you deserve a chance to make something of your life.'

I could feel the *but* coming up.

'…But I can't do any more. I don't want to be caught in the middle of a family feud. I don't want anyone else to know what I've done.'

I hung my head. 'I understand,' I said. And I did – but my heart sank. I had hoped that maybe I could talk to her from time to time, ask her advice.

'So you don't want me to contact you?'

'Not just now,' she said gently. 'Once this is all resolved, once the dust has settled, then of course you can. You can come back and see me. But right now, I think it's best we don't keep in touch.'

She looked at her watch and got up. 'I must go,' she said briskly.

She hugged me briefly and then she was gone. Her car was parked outside the main entrance and I stared out of my window down on to it. I watched her run down the front steps, the sun catching briefly on her watch face. Then she unlocked the car and got inside. She glanced up once at my window and waved, then started the engine and drove away down the long drive.

I watched until the car was out of sight, and then I turned slowly away from the window.

I had never, in my entire life, been so alone.

The solitude was overwhelming. I poured myself a glass of water and then dragged my mobile out of my pocket. Already there was a missed call. I saw that it was from Asma, so I listened to it. Her voice was angry.

'Where *are* you, Halima? Ammi's worried sick. Call me as soon as you pick this up.'

I composed a text, choosing my words very carefully.

I'm safe and happy but I'm not going to Khalil's wedding and I'm not going to marry the man Baba's chosen for me.

It was bald, but it was the truth. What else could I say?

Don't try calling me. I won't answer. Text if you like.

I was about to send it, and an image of Ammi came into my head. My poor Ammi, shocked and miserable, torn between her love of me and her unquestioning obedience to Baba. I added another sentence. *And please tell Ammi that I love her.*

Then, before I lost my nerve, I sent it, with my free hand wiping away the tears which were coursing down my cheeks.

And then, immediately, I sent a text to Kate.

I've done it! I'm safe. Have a great trip. See you next term.

Brave words. But my mood was anything but triumphant.

I switched off my mobile and searched in my

luggage for the little prayer mat I had brought with me. I took it out and laid it carefully on the floor of my room. Then I went into my bathroom and washed carefully, the familiar ritual calming me.

No one disturbed me. I made the set prayers and then added some special ones of my own, asking Allah to protect me, to protect my family and to give me strength.

When I'd finished, I wondered whether I'd be able to visit the nearest mosque. It was in Oxford, which was a long bus journey and one I probably couldn't afford until I got a job. I opened up my laptop to check how to get there. Thank goodness I had brought the laptop. Otherwise, anyone could have tracked my recent searches and worked out where I was. I'd looked up Oxford mosques online, I'd visited the college website numerous times, and I'd sent masses of emails to Kate. Even though I'd been careful to trash them immediately, anyone with a bit of computer knowledge would have been able to retrieve them.

I had covered my tracks carefully and I was sure no one would be able to find me.

Slowly I began to unpack my bags. There was no hurry. I had all the time in the world. There was no one to talk to. I was quite alone.

Very carefully I took my wedding *dupatta* from

my backpack. It was only half finished; perhaps I would work on it here. I picked it up and ran the chiffon through my fingers. Such a delicate thing, and it would be so beautiful when it was finished. I sighed. I'd probably never wear it now.

A lump rose in my throat. Handling the veil took me right back to the village in Pakistan, and I could see so clearly Ammi's head bent over, showing me how to stitch when I was little, handing down her own skill to me. My tears spilled on to the veil as I placed it carefully on the table beside my bed.

Gradually I made the room my own. I put my laptop on the desk under the window, I put my washing things in the bathroom, hung my few clothes in the wardrobe and stacked my books carefully on the shelves.

I'd not had room to bring bed linen. There was a rather flat duvet on the bed but no cover or undersheet, and no towels.

Suddenly, this little detail unnerved me and I sat on the bed and put my head in my hands.

I must be strong.

Eventually, I got up and went back downstairs to the Principal's office. As I walked over the wooden floors in the hall, my footsteps sounded loud in the silence.

I knocked on the door but there was no response. I tried turning the handle, but it was locked.

As I was standing there, someone came past –

a middle-aged woman carrying a load of files. She smiled at me. 'Can I help?'

I explained, haltingly, about my lack of bedclothes. I was waiting for the questions – what was I doing here, why was I here during the vacation – but the woman said, 'Wait a minute. I'll see what I can do.'

Then she put down her files, opened up the Principal's office, picked up the files again and went inside.

'What's your room number?' she asked.

I shook my head. My brain was so numb, I had already forgotten.

'It'll be on your key.'

I fished the key out of my pocket and showed it to her.

'OK,' she said. 'Leave it with me. The housekeeper's out, but I'll get her to bring things up to you later.'

I hung around, not knowing what to do.

'Anything else I can help you with?'

'Er, yes. Where do I get the bus into town?'

The woman gave me the information I needed, but she clearly wanted get on with her work, so I thanked her and crept back upstairs to my room. I didn't feel brave enough yet, to take the bus into town. Maybe soon.

CHAPTER EIGHTEEN

Mahmood

I only found out by accident. I knew that Halima's parents and brother had left for Pakistan, for the wedding, and I thought that Halima had gone with them. I kept imagining her with this guy. I was beating myself up for being so weak. Why hadn't I stopped her going? Now she was probably already engaged to the man.

I'd been to see Habib and Asma but they said nothing about Halima – they just said that the rest of the family had left for Pakistan.

Then one evening I called in unexpectedly. Habib let me into the flat and I could hear Asma talking loudly on the phone in the other room.

'What can I do, Ammi?' she yelled. 'She won't speak to me.' Then silence. 'No. I told you! I have no idea where she is.'

Habib steered me into the kitchen but I could still hear Asma, her voice raised in irritation.

I looked at Habib. 'What's happened?'

He was embarrassed and wouldn't meet my eyes. 'Nothing. Just some family trouble.' He shrugged. 'You know how it is.'

Suddenly I realised why he was being so shifty. *Family trouble.* I took him by the shoulders and forced him to look at me. 'Is it Halima? Has something happened to her?'

'No, no. Nothing like that...'

'Don't lie to me, Habib!' I was angry now and sure I was right. 'That's who Asma's talking about, isn't it?'

Habib didn't answer.

'What's happened to her? Is she in trouble?'

Habib gestured towards the closed door. 'Shhh,' he said. 'You'll upset Asma.'

But at that moment Asma came out. She was flushed and obviously upset. When she saw me, she started.

'Mahmood! I didn't know you were here.'

I dispensed with the niceties. 'Asma, what's happened?'

'What do you mean?'

Habib moved towards her and put his arm round her shoulders. 'It's OK, Mahmood, it's nothing.'

They were presenting me with a wall of silence, but I wouldn't leave it alone. I brushed aside his remark. 'It's Halima, isn't it? Something's happened to her?'

Asma frowned. 'She decided not to go to Pakistan,' she said. 'That's all. She needed to study.'

'What a load of bullshit!' I yelled. 'She's run away, hasn't she?'

Asma looked up at me then, and her eyes were full of tears.

'She has, hasn't she?'

Asma nodded miserably.

'You're not to tell anyone, Mahmood,' said Habib. 'You understand?'

'Oh yes, I understand,' I said bitterly. 'I understand all right.'

'She'll come back. I'm sure she'll come back,' said Asma. 'She doesn't want to leave her family.'

'And what about the guy in Pakistan?'

Habib frowned. 'She's promised to him. You know that. I told you, Mahmood.'

I lost my temper then. 'This is barbaric, Habib. For God's sake, you've lived here long enough. No girl should be forced to marry someone against her will.'

Asma interrupted. 'She never said she wouldn't marry him, Mahmood.'

'No, of course she didn't. Think of the trouble! Think what your father would do! Instead, she's run away because she can't stand the thought of being with some man she's never met, doesn't respect and who thinks she's owed to him.'

In the silence that followed, the baby started crying and Asma fled out of the room. Habib scowled at me.

When Asma came back, she was cradling the baby in her arms and tears were running down her cheeks.

'Have you spoken to her?' I asked gently.

Asma shook her head. 'She won't answer her phone. But she sends me texts. She says she's safe.'

I cursed myself, then, for not getting Halima's phone number from her. But she probably wouldn't have given it to me.

'If you give me her number, ' I began. 'Perhaps...'

'No!' said Asma sharply. 'This is our business, Mahmood. Our family's business. If you interfere, you will only make things worse for her.'

Shortly after that, I left and went to the park. I paced round and round, trying to think of how I could contact her.

I wanted her to know I cared for her. I wanted her to know I admired her and what she'd done. But Asma might be right. I could make things a lot worse for her.

Where was Halima now? What was she doing? How would she manage on her own?

CHAPTER NINETEEN

Halima

The days dragged by. I had never felt so lonely in my life. The college had conferences during the vacation and business people came and went, held meetings, ate meals, but they were bound up in their own concerns and no one noticed me.

There was a small café on the campus and I bought food there and ate it alone in my room, staring at the four walls. I tried to study but every so often my mind would freeze up and my thoughts would go back, again and again, to what I had done. How would Ammi be taking it? I knew she'd be worried about me and I hated making her unhappy. And Baba? He'd just be furious that I had messed up his wonderful plan for me.

Most days I walked in the grounds speaking to nobody, watching people come and go. It got so that I became scared of leaving the safety of the campus, but one day I told myself that I must stop this. I must get out. I needed money. I needed work.

My savings wouldn't last much longer.

Eventually I screwed up my courage and went to look around the nearest town, taking the bus which stopped outside the college. No one was talking when I got on the bus and I felt that everyone was staring at me. But, being English, they soon looked away. I really stood out here. How different from Walthamstow, where every other person in our street was Pakistani. I decided then that I must make myself less conspicuous. I would leave off my *hijab* in future and buy some jeans and tops at a charity shop. I must try and blend in. I mustn't be so easy to spot.

As the bus lumbered towards the town, I looked around me. The countryside was in full bloom, the leaves still that wonderful acid green of early summer before the heat makes them tired, and the wheat in the fields still unripened. It was a glorious day and I felt my spirits lift. When we reached the middle of the town, I got out, together with most of the other passengers.

I walked slowly down the high street, peering into the shop windows. Everything was different. The clothes, the food, the pace of life. It was a small town with a wide main street and old buildings, some of them uneven and some timbered. It felt timeless and gentle and very English.

I found a charity shop and bought a couple of

pairs of jeans and some tops for practically nothing. I emerged from the shop with my hair swinging free and my usual clothes bundled into a plastic bag. I smiled. Ammi would have been horrified.

Then I went into a café and sat there drinking a coffee and wondering whether I had the courage to walk into a shop and ask if they had a part-time job.

I made my coffee last as long as I could – until it was cold in the cup. The waitress came over and asked if I wanted another. My thoughts were so far away that I jumped. I'd almost forgotten how to chat, how to exchange normal everyday pleasantries.

I blushed. 'No. No, thank you.' She started to walk away. I summoned up my courage. 'Excuse me.'

She turned back. 'Yes?'

'I'm... er... I want to do some work here over the summer. Do you now where I can look for a job?'

She frowned. 'What sort of work?'

'I've worked in a dress shop,' I said. 'But anything really. I don't mind what I do.'

She smiled at me then. 'If you go into the supermarket,' she said, 'they have a noticeboard there. There are cards advertising jobs.'

I got up. 'Thanks a lot. I'll go and look now.'

She started to wipe the table. 'You could be lucky. Schools haven't broken up yet, so there might be something – before the school leavers snap them up.'

I thanked her again. She smiled. 'No problem. Let me know if you have any luck.'

'Yes. I will.'

A friendly face, a smile. Suddenly I felt more welcome in this place, less of a stranger.

I walked slowly down the road. I had plenty of time. The bus didn't go back past the college for another hour. I walked through the automatic doors of the supermarket and immediately saw the noticeboard at the front of the shop near the kiosk selling cigarettes and lottery tickets. I read the cards pinned up there.

Bar work. I smiled to myself. However desperate I was, I certainly wouldn't work where alcohol was served. I really would be an outcast if I did!

Sales assistant in newsagent. Possible, I suppose.

Sales assistant in clothing store. Definitely possible.

Babysitting. Not sure about that. I'd rather not get involved with a family. They'd ask too many questions.

I scribbled down the phone numbers of the two possibles and then went out into the street again. In a quiet doorway I phoned the clothing store.

I was terrified the shop would want a reference from where I'd worked in Walthamstow. They'd certainly give me one, but the people who ran the place knew my family and they'd be sure to let on where I was. But the woman who interviewed me seemed satisfied when I told her I was a student at the local college, and half an hour later, I had a job! Only two afternoons a week, but that was all I needed. And I could keep it up when term started. I was sure I could juggle it somehow.

Before I went back, I popped in to see the waitress in the café. She was serving but she spotted me at the door. 'Any luck?' she mouthed. I nodded and grinned. She gave me a thumbs-up sign.

The driver smiled at me as I boarded the bus. I'm sure he didn't recognise me as the girl in the *hijab* who had got on earlier. The bus was full and I squeezed in next to a large lady with a shopping bag on her lap. She smiled at me, too.

It was with a lighter heart that I walked up the long drive to college. I had a job. It wasn't much, but it meant I could afford to eat – and I'd be seeing people and talking to them.

Slowly, day by day, my mind began to unfreeze. I liked the people who came into the shop. Mothers with children, businesswomen, grannies. Sometimes they talked to me and asked me what I was doing. My answer was always the same. I was at the college and I was staying during the summer to study, while my family was in Pakistan.

But I longed for the company of people my own age. There was a long time to go before term started.

I often thought of Imran and one day, while I was alone in my room at college, I rang him.

'Hey, little sister. What's up? Where are you? I heard all about it. Are you OK?'

It was the first time I'd heard the voice of any member of my family for ages and I felt a great surge of longing.

'It's so good to hear you!' I said. 'Are you OK?'

'Yeah. I'm OK. But tell me where you are, Halima. Let's meet up, eh?'

I paused. Could I trust him with my secret? Better not.

'Imran, I'm a long way from Walthamstow, but I'm safe and I'm studying.'

'Studying? How come? Where?'

'I've transferred. But... but I can't tell you where I am.'

There was a pause, then, 'Yeah. I understand. Though I'd never tell them, Halima. I'd never let on.'

I thought back to the arrogant Imran I'd known, to the cocksure young man, certain of his male superiority. He sounded gentler now. He had changed.

He was speaking again. 'You know, there've been rumours, Halima.'

'Rumours? About me?'

'Sort of.'

I felt a tiny prick of fear. 'What, Imran? What are they saying?'

'Well, you know Baba told everyone in Pakistan that you'd stayed in England to study?'

'Yes, Asma sent me a text.'

He paused again. 'Well, it seems that this guy you're supposed to be marrying didn't believe it. And he insisted on speaking to you himself.'

'Ah.'

'Yes – awkward for Baba, as you can imagine, seeing as he knew you wouldn't answer your mobile and you weren't living at home. He had to admit that you'd run away.'

'Where did you hear this, Imran?'

'From Habib.'

I frowned at the mobile in my hand. 'But you've never met Habib, Imran. You weren't living at home when he came on the scene.'

Imran chuckled. 'I have met him. I know him through friends and we speak quite often, though Asma doesn't know. She wouldn't want him getting too friendly with her no-good brother.'

I sighed. How long would it be before Asma froze me out of her life, too?

Imran went on. 'But that's not all, little sister.'

'What do you mean?'

'The guy's father is really angry. I mean, *really* angry.'

My heart started beating a little faster and I gripped my phone hard.

Imran went on. 'He's furious, Halima and… and they think he might come looking for you.'

'What!'

'Listen, it's only a rumour and they may be saying that to frighten you into coming home.'

'Who? Who's saying that?'

'The family.'

'You mean Baba?'

'Yes. He's pretty angry, too.'

I swallowed. 'Imran,' I said quietly. 'I'm not coming home. I'm happy here. I'm going to study and get my degree. And then I'm going to get a good job.'

'I admire you, little sister, believe me. But you'll be doing it on your own. And you'll have to make very sure no one can find you.'

'I know,' I said.

We chatted on for a while and he seemed pleased to talk to me – really talk, in the way we never used to when we were at home together. We spoke about Baba and Ammi and how we were moving away from their way of thinking. Imran couldn't understand why Baba was giving me a good education and then forcing me into a marriage I didn't want. Surely, he said, Baba must realise that I had a mind of my own.

'He's got no choice, Imran. At least, that's how he sees it. He promised, so he must deliver.'

'He should never have put you in this position.'

'Well, I suppose, when he made the promise, things were different.'

'Don't tell me you're feeling sorry for him!'

I laughed. 'No! Well, not really. But I can see how difficult it is for him.'

It was such a relief to speak to a member of my family who didn't try to make me change my mind. I could relax with Imran, and he made me feel better about what I had done.

'Imran,' I said. 'You know I'd really really like to see you, but just now…'

'No, I understand. Better not let anyone know where you are.'

'You will speak to me again?'

'I'll speak to you any time. You know that.'

'I'll phone you again soon, then,' I said. 'And Imran…'

'Yeah?'

'Thanks.'

'What for?'

'For warning me.'

'That's OK. But you be careful, Halima. Look after yourself, little sister.'

I switched off my mobile and sat on the edge of my bed. Why hadn't Asma told me any of this? Although I'd not spoken to her, we'd sent each other texts regularly. In every one of them, she'd begged me to come home, told me I was making trouble for the family, but she'd never said anything about someone coming after me. Maybe she didn't want to frighten me. Maybe she didn't know. But if Habib knew, then surely...

Or maybe she wanted me to be caught. Was that it? Did she want me to cave in and do what Baba wanted so that the family honour would stay intact?

Did she want me found at any price?

I couldn't believe that my lovely sister Asma would wish any harm to come to me but then, more than anything, she wanted harmony in the family. Imran had gone, but Khalil had bent to Baba's will. Asma wanted me to do the same.

I felt really depressed after talking to Imran and I almost wavered, almost wondered whether I had done the right thing. Here I was, without friends of my own age, lonely, estranged from the family. Was it really all worth it?

But then I heard those words again.

You are owed me.

And the moment I thought what my life might be like with the guy from Saudi, I knew I was right,

I couldn't do it. But the news from Imran was chilling. Surely no one could track me down here, could they? And if they wanted to bundle me out of the country, force me to go to Saudi and marry the guy, they'd have to have my passport, wouldn't they? And Baba had my passport.

Thoughts kept whirling round my brain. Perhaps they knew people who could supply a false passport. Perhaps they'd employ someone to track me down – like a private detective.

Oh, stop it, I told myself. Stop being so hysterical. You are safe. You are being extremely careful. No one except Kate and Miss Brunner knows where you are. The guy in Saudi will soon forget you. Why would he want you now, anyway? You're not exactly ideal wife material.

I longed to see Kate again and tell her everything. I'd sent her a few texts but phoning mobile-to-mobile was expensive to America and I knew she was having a great time. I didn't want to ruin her holiday by worrying her.

For a few days after speaking to Imran, every man I saw looked suspicious. Was that man walking behind me in town a private dectective? And what about the fellow at the back of the bus? And who was the man pacing round the college campus with his hands behind his back?

I told Imran of my fears the next time I phoned him. 'That's good, little sister. Go on being suspicious. Don't drop your guard.'

And then he said something that made me forget everything about being followed.

'I met a friend of yours the other day.'

'Oh yeah. Who?'

'A guy called Mahmood.'

I tried to sound cool, but my heart started beating so fast that it banged against my ribs. 'Oh... him. Yes, he's a cousin of Habib's. Where did you meet him?'

'At my friend's house.'

'Is he... did he ask after me?' I tried not to sound too eager.

Imran laughed. 'Once he found out I was your brother, he never stopped asking after you! You've certainly made a conquest there, Halima!'

I couldn't pretend any more. 'Oh Imran, what shall I do?'

'Do you like him?'

I sighed. 'I've only met him twice but yes, I really like him. He made me realise that there are Pakistani men out there who don't think like Baba.'

'Yeah, he's a good bloke.' He hesitated. 'He wanted your phone number.'

'Did you give it to him?'

'No, of course not. I wouldn't do that!'

I felt the tears coming. 'Oh Imran. I wish you had. It would be so good to talk to him again. And what harm could it do now? I've already broken away from the family, so I'm hardly being conventional – and I need all the friends I can get.'

Imran didn't say anything for a moment, then he went on. 'It probably wouldn't do him much good to contact you, Halima. Just think about it from his point of view. He'd be talking to someone who has disgraced her family. How do you think his family would react?'

'I don't know. I have thought about it and that's why I've tried to put him out of my mind. I don't want to make trouble for him. But... well his family's been here for two generations. I think they might understand. And if it hadn't been for this stupid debt of honour, Baba would think him really suitable for me. After all, he's had a good education, comes from a good family, ticks all the boxes.'

'I feel really sorry for you, little sister. I got out because I couldn't stand the pressure from Baba. I've only got myself to blame. But you, you're different.'

'We're in the same situation, though.'

'I know. So, just in case you wanted it, guess what I've got?'

'What?'

'*His* number.'

I laughed, my spirits soaring. 'You're a star!'

'At least that gives you the option. If you want to contact him, you can. But don't do anything without thinking it through.'

As soon as I put the phone down, I entered Mahmood's number in my mobile. I looked at it. I wouldn't phone him yet. Imran was right. I needed to think carefully about it. I'd feel awkward making the running, but it was wonderful to have the number there, to know that I could hear his voice again.

I continued to keep a lookout for stalkers but then, as each day followed the next and nothing happened, I started to feel more relaxed. I enjoyed my two afternoons at the dress shop. The manager was pleased with me and started to give me more responsibility.

And it wasn't too long, now, before the beginning of term. When term began again, I would blend into the crowd – I would be just another student, a pile of books under my arm, attending lectures, chatting to friends or glued to my mobile.

CHAPTER TWENTY

I watched from my window as the students started to return to college. I was jealous of those being dropped off by their families, greeting their friends with loud shrieks, thundering up the stairs, slamming doors, playing music.

Suddenly the whole place came alive. I was so used to the solitude that I found it unnerving at first, and I was very shy. Everyone seemed to know each other and I thought I wouldn't fit in.

But I was wrong. Right from the first day they were friendly – and particularly the two Muslim students doing the same course as me. I'd been scared that the work would be different – harder, unfamiliar – but because I'd had so much time to study during the holiday, I was well ahead. I began to relax and feel part of it all again. My lonely days were behind me – at least for now.

Kate phoned me as soon as she was back from America and we arranged to meet up.

'I'm really broke, Kate. I'm not sure that I can

afford the fare to Oxford.'

'Don't worry. I'm coming to see you!'

'Hey, that's great. When?'

'Is next Saturday afternoon OK with you?'

I hesitated. 'I'm working in the afternoon, at the dress shop. Could you come in the morning?'

'Mmm. Morning's no good – I'm doing something then, but I could meet you when you've finished work.'

We arranged to meet in the café in the early evening. For the first time, I was really anxious for my shift at the shop to end and then, of course, a customer came in just before closing time. She was really slow, taking ages trying on one outfit after another. I tried to be patient, but I was watching the clock as I waited for her to decide, and then I wrapped up her purchase with fumbling fingers. But at last I was free to go and I raced down the high street and into the café.

And there she was, the same as ever. Bright eyes, wild hair, crazy clothes and a huge grin. As soon as I walked in, she rushed over to me and gave me a hug. Then she held me away from her.

'Hey, who's this Western girl? Where's the scarf? And what's with the jeans? You look almost normal!' She fished out a digital camera from her bag and took a photo. 'This I have to have on record!'

I laughed, and introduced her to my friend in the café.

'She's the lady who got me the job,' I said.

Kate smiled at her. 'A friend in need, eh?'

We ordered our drinks and talked and talked. I heard all about Kate's trip to the States, about her friends at Oxford, her boyfriend, her course, the funny traditions they have there. She made it all sound great.

'Thanks for trekking over here, Kate. Next time, I'll try and make it to Oxford. I really want to see it – and I want to go to the mosque there, too. It's ages since I've been.'

'You'd love Oxford,' she said. 'But hey, it'll keep. Now, tell me about you. What's happening with the runaway daughter?'

'Not bad. I'm doing OK with the work and I like it here.'

'What about your family?'

I made a face. 'I talk to Imran.'

Then I told her what Imran had said about the Saudi guy's father being so angry and perhaps coming to find me.

Kate looked serious. 'That's a bit sinister, isn't it? But Halima, there are laws about that sort of thing in this country. This is England. No one can kidnap you.'

I shrugged. 'Don't be too sure. I've dishonoured his family. But I'm hoping he won't want me for his son now. I'm hoping he'll think I'm too much trouble.'

'What does Asma think about it?'

'I don't speak to Asma. I text her, but she wants me to come home and marry the guy. I can't talk to her. She'll put pressure on me to tell her where I am. Then, when I refuse, she'll get upset and so will I.'

Kate took a long drink of her coffee. Suddenly she grinned. 'And what about the boyfriend – Mahmood, was it?'

'Kate, he's not a boyfriend. Well, not in the way you mean.'

And then I told her that Imran had met him and that I was screwing up my courage to phone him.

'What's stopping you?'

I rolled my eyes. 'You know what's stopping me!'

She laughed. 'Your upbringing, that's all! You should contact him, Halima. He obviously cares about you.'

'Maybe. I don't know. It's complicated.' I changed the subject. 'We'll have to go soon, Kate. They're closing up.'

'But there's so much I want to tell you. Why don't I come back to college with you and stay the night in your room? That would be OK, wouldn't it? I can get the bus back to Oxford in the morning.'

'Yeah… I guess so. But there's only one bed.'

'Oh don't worry about me. I'm happy on the floor.'

'Well…'

'Come on, Halima. It's Saturday night, for goodness sake. You're a free agent now. You can do what you want.'

'I suppose so,' I said doubtfully. There was no stopping her. She'd made up her mind and I trailed along in her wake.

'I saw a supermarket down the road,' she said, standing up and pulling me to my feet. 'We can get something to eat there and take it back to your room. I'll get a bottle of wine and...'

'Wine? Hang on Kate,' I said, laughing.

'Oh yeah. Just slipped my mind for a moment.'

We walked arm in arm down the high street and into the supermarket, chatting and laughing. I felt so happy. I glanced up at the notices by the door where I'd seen the card advertising the job in the dress shop.

If I had glanced the other way, if I had looked over my shoulder, I would have seen him.

Neither of us knew it, but he had been waiting a long time. Waiting for his opportunity. He had followed Kate from Oxford. He had been sitting in the café all the time we were there, reading a newspaper, hidden from view behind a large pot plant.

He came into the supermarket after us and neither of us noticed him.

The supermarket was crowded with shoppers getting their last minute weekend food.

'I'll get stuff for dinner,' said Kate. 'My treat.'

'OK. I'll go and buy some milk.'

We separated. I went down the aisle to the dairy section, Kate went over to the delicatessen.

I was bending over, picking a carton out of the chiller cabinet, when I felt someone jostle me. And then I felt a stab of pain as something was plunged into my arm. I remember whipping round and seeing a man's face up close. A Pakistani man.

And then everything went black.

CHAPTER TWENTY-ONE

Kate

It happened so fast. I was talking to the lady behind the deli counter, asking her to make sure the quiche had no bacon in it, when, out of the corner of my eye, I saw some people leaning over a figure huddled on the floor in another aisle.

'What's going on?' I asked the deli lady.

'Dunno. Looks like someone's fainted. Not surprising. There's always such a crowd here on a Saturday.'

I took the quiche and turned away, strolling back towards the dairy counter to find Halima. The girl who had fainted was being carried out by a young man, and at first I didn't notice who she was.

Then I spotted her top. The charity shop top she'd been so proud of.

'Halima!' I shouted.

I dropped the quiche and ran after them, pushing people aside in my hurry. People swore at me, barred my path, but I fought my way through. The man had gone through the doors, and was carrying her outside.

'Halima!' I yelled again.

They were in the road by now.

Someone said to me, 'It's OK. She's with her brother.'

'Her brother?'

'Yes, the man's her brother. He said she often faints.'

For a moment I hesitated. Was Imran here – or Khalil? Surely not. She'd said none of her family knew where she was. I ran outside on to the pavement and saw the man bundling her into the back of a car.

The man was not her brother.

I turned to the little crowd of people behind me. 'That's not her brother!' I shouted. 'Stop him!'

But there was bewilderment on their faces and no one moved, so I raced across the road, dodging the traffic, and reached the car as it was pulling away from the kerb. I yanked at the back door, but it was locked. I banged on the windows, shouting and screaming at the driver to stop, but he took no notice and accelerated away, looking straight ahead. I ran after the car, and the tyres screamed as he pulled the wheel round and headed down the road. Several drivers had to brake sharply as he swerved and wove in and out of the traffic.

The number. I must get the car number.

I screwed up my eyes and tried to focus on the letters and numbers on the number plate. I repeated them to myself and then fumbled in my bag and found a scrap of paper and a biro. With trembling hands, I wrote them down before I forgot. Then I ran back to where the car had been, to the little knot of people who were standing there staring.

'What's the matter, love?' said someone as I came running back to them.

I was so out of breath that I could hardly speak. 'Get the police,' I gasped. 'Someone please call the police. She's been kidnapped. My friend's been kidnapped!'

I felt an arm round my shoulder. It was Halima's friend from the café.

'Calm down, love,' she said. 'What's this all about?'

I took a few deep breaths and tried to speak clearly. 'She's in danger,' I said quietly. 'Believe me, she's in real danger. I must speak to the police.'

'OK, come back to the café and we'll call from there.' Then she stooped down and picked something up from the ground. 'Here, you've dropped your phone.'

I felt in my pocket. My phone was still there. I looked at the mobile in the woman's hand and my heart missed a beat. It was Halima's. It must have fallen out of her pocket when she was being dumped in the car. Without her phone, she'd have no way of contacting me.

I took it from the woman and she gently led me back to the café. She had locked up for the night, but she let me in and we sat at one of the tables as I phoned the police.

The process was so slow.

'Can you come to the police station, Madam?'

'Well yes, I suppose so, but the longer we leave it...'

'Yes Madam, I understand your concern, but we'll need a statement.'

Why? Why did they need a statement? I'd given them the car number. Why couldn't they stop it?

I went on gabbling, the words spilling out. 'There was this man in the supermarket. He said she'd fainted and that he was her brother.'

'We'll check that out, Madam.'

'But he's not her brother. I've met her brothers!'

'If you can come to the station Madam, we'll take down all the details.'

I snapped my mobile shut and banged the table with frustration. 'That car could be anywhere by now. Anything could be happening to her.'

Then I felt a hand on my arm. 'Come on. We'll go to the police station,' said Halima's friend. 'It's not far.'

We ran all the way to the police station. The man on duty was calm and kind but I couldn't stand the fact that nothing was happening.

'We'll need her home address,' he said. 'Then we can check whether it was her brother.'

'But I'm telling you it wasn't! I've met her brothers.'

The policeman looked at me steadily. 'That may be so,' he said, 'but it could have been another relation. I'll speak to the family.'

'OK,' I said. I was sure that her family would be horrified at what had happened to her. Halima had always said that her father wouldn't want her harmed.

Slowly and methodically, the policeman took down the phone number of Halima's parents and went into another room. He was gone a long time, and I paced up and down, gnawing my nails. Halima's friend from the café kept coming up with soothing platitudes, which set my teeth on edge.

At last the policeman came back. He was smiling. 'I've spoken to her father,' he said, 'and it appears that her cousin came here on a surprise visit. She's with him, and they're on their way back to Walthamstow to spend the rest of the weekend with the family.'

'What? Her father said what?'

He repeated it.

I stared at him open-mouthed. 'And you believed

him? For God's sake, she ran away from home because her father wants to force her to marry some guy she's never met. Her parents didn't even know where she was. She doesn't want to go home. Don't you understand?' I was shouting now and I know I was sounding hysterical. 'Oh, please do something.'

There was silence and the man looked uneasy. For a moment I thought he might change his mind and try and help find her, but then he spoke again. 'Look, her father reassured me that she's safe and with a member of the family.'

And however much I ranted and raved, he was adamant that he wasn't going to take it any further.

It was getting late, and suddenly I couldn't bear to be stuck in the station any longer. If I hurried, I could catch the last bus back to Oxford. I wanted to be back in my room, among my sane friends, away from this madness. But most of all, I needed time to think.

I chose a seat on the bus at the back, well away from anyone else.

What should I do? I was absolutely sure that Halima's father was lying. But if he was, then he must know what was happening. He must have condoned this kidnap. Surely no father would do that to their daughter, would they?

How had they tracked her down? She'd been so careful.

And then I realised. Of course! It was through me! Her family knew how close we were. They probably thought I'd helped her run away and that I knew where she was. They guessed I'd contact her, so someone in her family must have given her abductor my name. Imran was right about a stalker. But the stalker must have been watching me, knowing that sooner or later I'd lead him to Halima. It would have been easy enough to track me down. I thought back to the article in the local paper and cursed.

'It's all my fault,' I muttered. 'I've messed everything up for her.'

As the bus rolled along in the autumn twilight, I tried to focus my thoughts. I felt so powerless – and so guilty.

I took Halima's phone out of my bag and started to scroll down her address book.

Asma. No, Halima wouldn't want me to contact her.

Imran. Well, he was the obvious one. Would he believe me? Would he help?

I took a deep breath and pressed the call button.

'Hi, little sister. How are you?'

'Imran. It's not Halima. I'm just using her phone. It's her friend from school. Kate. Do you remember me?'

'Er, yeah…'

'Look Imran. It's about Halima. She's... she's disappeared, and I'm really worried about her.'

'What? What's happened?'

I spoke fast, tripping over my words, giving him no chance to interrupt. 'I was shopping with her today in a supermarket. We were in different places and then the next thing I know, some guy is carrying her out of the shop saying he's her brother and she's fainted and he's taking her home...'

'Slow down, Kate. Take it easy. Did you get a look at the guy?'

'Yes. I saw him outside the supermarket and then getting into the car. I think I'd recognise him again.'

'Oh God,' said Imran quietly. 'I was so scared this would happen to her. Poor Halima.' He paused. 'What did you do then?'

'I ran out after them, but the man bundled her into a car and drove off – that's when her mobile fell in the road. I got the car number and I've been to the police and they phoned your father.'

'Good. I'm glad you've been to the police already. What did my father say to them.'

'Apparently, he said it was fine, that she was with her cousin and he knew all about it...'

'What! That can't be right! I'm sure my father wouldn't go along with a kidnap.'

There was an awkward silence. I didn't reply.

I didn't know what to think any more.

Imran cleared his throat. 'But how did the guy find her? She's been so careful. She wouldn't even tell me where she was living.'

'I think it was through me,' I said miserably. 'I guess someone's been watching me and they knew I'd lead them to her.' Suddenly I felt tired and desolate. 'Imran, we must do something. We must find her.'

'Of course. Of course we must find her. If we don't, she'll be taken out of the country and forced to marry this man from Saudi.'

'But she hasn't got a passport. She told me. Your father has it.'

Imran gave a dry laugh. 'That won't stop them,' he said. 'She's probably been kidnapped by a third party. Someone who's being paid well to find her. They won't worry about a genuine passport!'

Suddenly, the whole situation shifted subtly. My stomach clenched. Was he talking about an organised gang? A criminal gang? What was I getting myself into?

'I thought it was just a family thing,' I said nervously.

'Mm, said Imran. 'It may have started out that way, but when the family couldn't find her, couldn't persuade her, my guess is that the guy from Saudi – or his father – employed someone to track her down.'

'No!'

'Yeah. It's a murky business, Kate. There are people out there who do this for a living – track down Asian brides who have gone missing.'

My mouth was dry and I swallowed. 'What about your father?'

'I don't know any more,' he said. 'I didn't think he'd ever... I've no idea what goes on in his head. I just don't understand where he's coming from. He must know something about it, to say what he did on the phone.'

I was talking quietly at the back of the bus, just another girl chatting into her mobile. I glanced round at my fellow passengers but they took no interest in me. Suddenly I had an idea. I lowered my voice even more.

'Imran, there are women's refuges out there which help girls like Halima. I've read about them in the papers. Why don't we approach one of them?'

'Well, yeah. I suppose we could. Probably better if you do it, though. They might be suspicious if I did... you know, a member of her family – and a bloke.'

'Oh. OK. I'll try. But I can't do anything until I get home. I can't search online till I get back.'

'Where are you?'

'On a bus going back to Oxford.'

'Ah! So she's been living near Oxford, then?'

When I didn't answer, he went on, 'Look. We can't waste time. I'll make enquiries and get back to you with some contact numbers as soon as I can. Maybe there's someone in Oxford you can speak to.'

'OK, thanks. But hurry, Imran. We must track her down before she's taken out of the country.'

'I know. I'll be as quick as I can.'

I rang off and sat there, trying to arrange my thoughts into some sort of coherent order. I must stay calm. If the local police wouldn't take any action, then we would have to. And we would have to do it fast. As I was thinking, I was scrolling down Halima's contacts.

I came across one name and stopped.

Mahmood.

Should I phone him? Would she want me to? Was this interfering too much?

Hell, I thought, I'm already in this up to my armpits. She needs all the friends she can get right now, and I'm sure he'd want to know what was happening to her.

Before I lost my nerve, I pressed Call.

Please answer! Please don't go into voicemail.

The phone rang for ages. Then at last, the voice mail kicked in. "Hi, this is Mahmood. Sorry I can't answer your call right now. Leave a message and I'll get back to you."

'Damn,' I muttered, then spoke clearly into the phone. 'Mahmood, this is Kate. I'm a good friend of Halima's. She's in a lot of trouble. Please call me as soon as you pick this up. It's really important.'

Then I sat back in my seat and closed my eyes, waiting for Imran or Mahmood to ring back. I was too tense to relax.

For the moment, I could do nothing more. Not from the back of a bus speeding through the darkness towards Oxford.

CHAPTER TWENTY-TWO

Mahmood

When I picked up her message, I was elated. She had contacted me! Halima had contacted me, even though it was through someone else. Then, the next second I registered: she was in trouble. What sort of trouble? I imagined all sorts of horrible scenarios even as I was returning the call.

'Kate, it's Mahmood. What's happened?'

When she told me, it was as if a knife was twisting in my gut. How dare this guy abduct her! How dare he! She must be terrified. What was happening to her? I couldn't bear to think. Then I pulled myself together. I knew who Kate was. I remember seeing her at Habib and Asma's *valmina.* I remembered how friendly she'd been with Halima. Kate with the wild red hair and the big green eyes and the pale skin. It was impossible to miss her among all the Asian girls.

She was talking again. I was so numb with worry that it took me a moment to make sense of it.

'I've spoken to Imran,' she said. 'He's going to

give me contact numbers for people who can help and I'll ring them, try and explain. Go and see them if necessary.'

'What do you mean? Who?'

'There are women's refuges who help victims of forced marriages.'

'Oh, I see. Yeah. Yeah I guess that's one way we could go. But would they be able to act right away? We need to do something now.' Then the fog cleared and I started to think more clearly. 'What about the Government's Forced Marriage Unit?' I said.

'What? I don't know about that. How do I get on to them?'

'Leave it with me. They're sure to be online. I'll get hold of them and tell them what you've told me. But...'

'But what?'

'They might want to speak to you, too. After all, you're the only one who can describe the guy and the only one who knows exactly what happened.'

'If it helps get her back, I'll do anything.'

'So will I,' I said quietly. Then, raising my voice a little. 'Look, I'll get back to you just as soon as I have any news. And I'll get straight on to Imran, too, so we don't go over the same ground.'

'Thanks, Mahmood. I'll wait to hear, then. Bye.'

'Hang on, Kate. Where are you?'

'On a bus on my way back to Oxford. I'll be there in about ten minutes.'

'Oxford. OK. Well, I've got a car. If you need to get anywhere, I can help.'

'Thanks. And Mahmood?'

'Yeah?'

'I know it's hard for you to get involved in all this… what with Halima defying her family and all that, and you being related to Habib. I know it'll put you in a difficult position with your own family and everything.'

I smiled to myself. I was sure now, despite everything that had happened. 'Nothing would be as bad as losing Halima,' I said.

There was a brief silence, and then Kate replied, 'That's what I hoped you'd say.'

CHAPTER TWENTY-THREE

Kate

The bus swung into the depot and I shrugged my backpack on to my shoulders and got out. I was so glad I'd phoned Mahmood. His last remark reassured me. He did care about her – really care – enough to put himself in a tricky position with his family.

I walked briskly to my rooms in college, and even in my anxiety, I took a moment to look up at the ancient magnificent buildings which surrounded me. What secrets they had seen over the centuries, what intrigues and what plots. And how many great people had passed through this place. I was so lucky to be a part of it. But I felt angry, too, when I thought that some man had been here, lurking in the quadrangle, perhaps watching my every movement, presumably since the beginning of term.

He couldn't be sure that I'd contact Halima and go and see her. It was horrible to think that he'd been stalking me for days, just on the off-chance. He must have been very patient. And very determined.

And, no doubt, well paid for his patience and determination.

As I climbed the stone staircase up to my room, Halima's phone rang and I stopped and answered it.

It was Mahmood. 'Kate, I've got through to the Forced Marriage Unit and they've been really helpful. They say they'll have to act fast to stop her being taken out of the country and they've asked the police to put a trace on the car number you gave Imran. But they say it may be false. And they want to speak to you right away, to question you about the man and to get a detailed description.'

'Hey, that's great. They certainly don't hang around,' I said. 'OK, give me their number.'

Mahmood gave me their number and a contact name.

I reached my room and dropped my backpack on the floor, and as soon as I'd got my breath, I rang them.

I got through to a very efficient-sounding woman and she questioned me thoroughly about what had happened, but when I started explaining the family background, she cut me short. 'We are only concerned with the safety of the victim,' she said. 'We never get involved with families.' There was a pause. 'We'll let you know if we have any news.'

'Will they try and take her out of the country?'

'Yes, almost certainly. They may even be on the way to an airport now.'

'But surely it will take time to get tickets?'

'You'd be amazed at how quickly these people act. They may already have seats on a plane in another name and false passports. They may be able to get a standby flight. There are all sorts of ways of getting out of the country fast. But we have contacts with the airport police and with social workers at all the main airports. We'll make sure that they're all on the lookout for her.'

'Can I do anything to help?'

'Well, can you remember anything about the man who abducted her – any feature that marks him out? Your friend may be on a false passport, so if you can think of any way we can identify him, that would be very helpful. Though, of course, he may not be with her. He may have sent someone else.'

And with that I had to be satisfied. I rang Imran and Mahmood to bring them up to date, and waited...

I was exhausted. It was going to be a long night. I closed my eyes and tried to snatch a few minutes' sleep, but I couldn't settle. My stomach was churning and I kept picturing Halima, drugged and terrified, probably in the back of some car, being driven to an airport, her future determined by people who cared nothing for her, who knew nothing of her hopes and ambitions. Who had no interest in her feelings but only cared about what they could get from her when she was delivered as part of some fiendish bargain they had struck with the man in Saudi or his father.

Halima must know that I wouldn't just let it happen to her. Surely she knew I'd move heaven and earth to rescue her.

Hang in there, babe. Be strong. We're doing everything we can.

I tried to think calmly, to relive those few moments when I had seen her abductor. What had the guy looked like? Was there anything which would help identify him?

When I'd seen him outside the supermarket with Halima in his arms, I'd seen his profile. Then he'd run across the road to his car. There was nothing special that I could remember about the way he moved. And then, when he'd bundled her into the back of the car, I'd seen his face. I guess he was about forty, with slightly receding hair. Greasy black hair, I do remember that. And he was clean-shaven.

And when I was banging on the window trying to stop him moving off, he didn't look round. All I had seen was the back of his neck and his shoulders and arms and hands as he'd wrenched the wheel round and driven away.

There was something niggling away in the back of

my mind. Was it something about his arms, his neck, his shoulders, his hands? Again and again I tried to picture what it was that was different about him, but it was no good. Whatever it was that had impressed itself into my subconscious wouldn't be teased out.

Suddenly I felt hungry. How different this evening should have been! Halima and I should have been eating together, laughing together, swapping experiences as we ate the quiche in her room. Instead, I'd abandoned the quiche on the supermarket floor, and now I rummaged around in my room for bread and cheese to make myself a lonely sandwich.

The minutes crawled by. I ate my sandwich and made myself some strong black coffee. Then I paced up and down in my room waiting for the phone to ring.

I jumped when it rang. It was the woman from the Forced Marriage Unit again.

'The car's been spotted!' she said.

'What! That's brilliant!'

'Yes,' she said. 'Our contacts in the police have run checks and found out it was a false number-plate, and then they ran it through the computer for speeding and it came up!'

'Fantastic! When? Where?'

A couple of hours ago. It went through a speed camera in Hounslow.'

'Hounslow!'

'Yes,' said the woman.

'Hounslow,' I repeated. 'If they are based round Hounslow, then they're really close to Heathrow – aren't they?'

The woman said nothing.

'Oh God,' I said. 'Do you think she's on a plane already?'

'They won't waste any time,' she said grimly. 'But our contacts at Heathrow are on to it. They'll all be looking out for her. Have you a recent photo of her?'

'What? Yes, yes, I took some this afternoon.'

'Well, can you send one over to me right away, then I'll forward it to our contacts at Heathrow.'

'Sure. And... thanks so much for all you're doing.'

'We just want her safely back where she belongs,' said the woman. Then she rang off.

Please don't let it be too late, I thought.

I found the photo, a shot of Halima in the café, laughing, her eyes shining, pushing a stray lock of her long dark hair away from her forehead. Was that really only this afternoon? *We'll find you,* I whispered. Then I hit the Send button.

I phoned Imran. 'The car's been spotted in Hounslow,' I said.

'Hounslow! That means...'

'Yes. It's really close to Heathrow.'

There was silence. Then Imran said, 'Kate, if it's been spotted round there, then I think I should go to the airport – just in case. Mahmood will drive me. If there's any chance that she is there, I want to be there to look after her.'

'But so do I!'

There was a slight hesitation and I held my breath. Was he going to tell me not to interfere, after all I'd done?

There was some muttering and then I heard Mahmood speaking firmly in the background. 'Of course. Of course she must come.'

Imran was back. 'OK then. Mahmood says we can be with you in an hour.'

It was the slowest hour of my life. I walked around my room, I looked at the photos I'd taken that afternoon, tried to read, to take my mind off things, but I couldn't concentrate. At last the phone rang.

'We're just driving up the High Street, Kate. We'll pick you up outside your college.'

'I'll be right there.'

I heaved on my backpack again and ran across the quad, through the porter's lodge and arrived on the pavement just as the car drew up. I scrambled in and Mahmood did a U-turn in the High Street and headed back the way they had come.

Imran was on the phone, talking rapidly.

He acknowledged me, but went on talking. Mahmood was concentrating on getting out of the town, driving as fast as he dared as we headed up the hill past Oxford Brookes and towards the A40.

Imran snapped his mobile shut and drew the back of his hand over his eyes, then twisted round to speak to me. 'I've been talking to someone at the Unit again. They say these gangs are really clever, Kate. They'll have disguised her, probably given her a different passport. And if she's on a flight to Saudi there'll be dozens of women who look like her, wearing *hijabs* or even *burqas.* It would be impossible to identify her under a *burqa.*'

'But she'd resist. Halima would yell out, tell someone she was being abducted. She wouldn't just let them take her.'

'She might not be able to,' said Mahmood quietly. 'She's probably been given some weird drug and doesn't know what's happening to her. She's probably completely disoriented. And if she's wearing a *burqa,* no one will notice.'

'Mm,' said Imran. 'And we don't know what threats they've made. They may have said they'll harm her family if she doesn't co-operate – or harm you, Kate.'

This was alien territory for me. I'd never been under any sort of threat or in any real danger in my life. I suddenly felt horribly vulnerable.

We sped along the A40 in silence, each with our own thoughts. Then they were interrupted by the harsh tune on Imran's phone.

He spoke urgently into it and then turned to me. 'There's a flight leaving for Riyadh in forty minutes,' he said. 'But no one with Halima's name is booked on the flight.'

'That doesn't mean she's not on it,' said Mahmood.

We drove on in silence, each of us conscious that time was ticking on. It was getting late and the traffic wasn't heavy, so we made good progress.

I tried to concentrate again on Halima's abductor. The description I'd given was accurate, as far as it went. Dark, greasy hair, slightly receding, about forty, average height and build. But again, there was this niggling feeling that I had seen something unusual.

Imran put his free hand up to his mouth and started to chew his nails anxiously.

Nails!

Suddenly, I knew what it was. *A finger without a nail.*

'Wait!' I yelled. 'There was something. I've just remembered.'

'What?' said Imran and Mahmood together.

I was staring at Imran's little finger.

'The guy who took Halima. His hand. The top of

his little finger was missing,' I said.

'Are you sure?'

I nodded. 'Quite sure.'

Mahmood turned to Imran. 'This may have nothing to do with anything,' he said slowly, 'but there was a guy like that at Habib's wedding. He was speaking to your father, Imran. And then he was hanging around when I was talking to Halima. We both saw his hand. We both noticed.'

'So, if it is him,' said Imran slowly, 'My father knows him.'

'It's probably just coincidence,' said Mahmood feebly.

'It's probably not,' said Imran.

There was a heavy silence. Imran sighed. 'I can't believe he'd get involved in this,' he muttered to himself. Then he said. 'Kate, you'd better get back to the Unit and let them know what you've told us.'

I should have felt elated when I realised that this could identify the guy but, looking at Imran's face, I could only feel terribly sad. Sad that any respect for his father had finally been shattered.

I wasn't on the phone for long and when I'd finished, I spoke to the boys. 'They think they may know who he is,' I said quietly.

'Hey, that's great – isn't it?' said Mahmood.

I nodded. 'If he's who they think he is, then

he's part of a gang which they've been trying to get evidence against for some time. A gang that gets paid for kidnapping Asian brides who run away. I just hope the police can get there in time and arrest him.'

'Don't get your hopes up Kate,' said Imran. 'We don't know that Halima is on a flight. We don't know that the guy is on the flight. He may not be travelling himself. If Halima is on the plane, she may be with someone else.'

As Mahmood hit the M25, the atmosphere was tense and none of us spoke much, but at last he was driving down the slip-road towards the airport. The airport itself was several miles from the turn-off, and it was taking so long. I kept looking at my watch. The minutes were ticking away. Even if we got there before the flight left, what could we do? We had no authority. All we could do was pray that if she was on the flight she'd been taken off.

'Which terminal?' asked Mahmood tersely.

'Four,' said Imran.

Mahmood drove as fast as he dared, but there was a queue of cars going into the short term car park.

'Get out!' he said to Imran. 'Go and check Departures.'

'I'm coming too,' I said, unbuckling my seat belt and leaping out of the back seat.

We ran across the road, dodging the taxis which

were dropping passengers off to catch their flights, and headed for Departures. The revolving door was too slow. I tried to push it, to make it speed up, but it made no difference.

Then at last we were through. Wildly I looked around for the screen listing the departures but even when I saw it, I was in such a state that I couldn't spot the flight.

'Imran,' I said, pointing to the screen. 'I can't see it.'

He screwed up his eyes and stared at the screen. 'Gate closed,' he said. 'That means it's about to take off.'

We ran to the departure barrier and found a policeman. Desperately, I tried to explain, but the words came out garbled. The policeman listened politely and then, with agonising slowness, he spoke on his walkie-talkie. When he'd finished, he turned to me.

'Come with me, Miss.'

'Where are you taking her?' said Imran. 'I want to come, too.'

'No, sir. They only want to see her,' said the man.

'Who?'

'My colleagues,' he said shortly. Then, to Imran. 'Stay here, sir, please.'

Bemused, I followed the policeman. He took me

to an interview room and left me there. There was another policeman in the room who gestured for me to sit down. It was a stark room with just a table and two chairs. The policeman sat on one side of the table and I sat on the other.

'You are here about a possible abduction?' he asked.

'Yes. The Government's Forced Marriage Unit knows all about it. We've been talking to them.'

'Yes. They've been in touch with us. And you say you witnessed the abduction?' he asked.

I nodded. 'My friend – the victim… the victim was with me when it happened.'

'Can I see some ID?'

With fumbling hands, I dug in my backpack and took out my student card. The policeman looked at it and then handed it back.

He seemed in no hurry. He went over everything I had already told the forced marriage people. He questioned me minutely about the man who had taken Halima: his build, his deformed finger, his age and so on – about the car, about the timing.

There was a clock on the wall of the interview room. As I answered his questions, I watched the hands move on. If she was on that flight, it was too late now to get her off it. If it was on time, it would have left by now. Once she was in Saudi Arabia, getting her back would be much much harder. She would be married immediately and once married, she would be living as a virtual prisoner of her husband. Even I knew how impossible it would be to get her out. And who knew what she been threatened with if she refused to marry?

What a mess. We had tried our best, Imran, Mahmood and I. We had done everything we could. Would the police or the Forced Marriage Unit be able to do anything once Halima was on the plane – or in Saudi?

I sat back in my chair defeated. It was all my fault. I had been such an idiot. I should have realised they'd try and get to her through me...

I was so wrapped up in my thoughts that I had to ask the policeman to repeat what he had just said.

'I said, would you be able to identify this man?'

I frowned. Were they going to fly me to Saudi Arabia? 'Well yes, I think so. Yes, I'm sure I can.'

He scraped back his chair and stood up. 'Good. Well, Kate, I'm glad to say that we have the man you describe in custody, and in due course you'll be asked to identify him formally.'

I started to shake. 'You mean he's here? He's been detained?'

The policeman nodded. 'We took him and his companion off the flight before it left.'

My heart was pounding against my ribs. So he *was* on the flight. And with Halima!

'He's known to us,' said the policeman, 'and to the Forced Marriage Unit. Until now, we have had nothing to charge him with, but if we can pin this one on him, then I think that he and his gang are finished. Hopefully, he'll get a long sentence and then be deported. And hopefully, when they see he's in custody, some of his other victims will be brave enough to come forward. We're beginning to break this thing down, Kate. These are criminals, these people who abduct young girls and boys to order. And the sooner they realise that they aren't above the law, the better.'

'And his companion?'

The policeman frowned. 'I have no doubt she is your friend, but at first she said that she was his wife – and her passport confirmed this.'

'What!'

The policeman smiled at me. 'It may be that she really is his wife. Or it may be that she has been threatened so that she'll say anything. But if she is your friend and she has been abducted, then we need her to press charges, and we need you to identify the man who abducted her, too. Unless that happens, then there's not a lot we can do.'

'She must be really scared about something to lie to you,' I muttered. Then I said. 'Can I see her?

I can certainly identify her and she won't pretend with me.'

He nodded. 'That's what I want you to do.'

I got up and followed him down a long corridor. We stopped outside a door and I started to shake. What if it wasn't her? What if it was some other luckless girl? Maybe it really was the guy's wife.

I took a deep breath when the policeman opened a door off the corridor.

Halima was sitting in a chair, eyes cast down, when I entered the room. A policewoman was with her. She'd obviously been dressed in a *burqa*, because it was draped across the back of her chair. I was about to rush forward, when the policeman put a firm hand on my arm. 'I want her to recognise you,' he whispered. 'Just to be sure.'

I stood – and waited.

Slowly, she raised her eyes. They were tear-stained and ringed with dark circles. She seemed to take ages to focus on my face.

'Kate?' she whispered, frowning.

The policeman let me go. I stumbled towards her and wrapped her in my arms. She was sobbing now, clinging to me. I started to cry, too.

At last I held her away from me and turned to the policeman.

'This is Halima,' I said, smiling through my tears.

He nodded at me. He was smiling too.

The policewoman touched my arm. 'She's been through a lot,' she said quietly. 'She's still very confused.'

Halima started talking slowly, haltingly. She held my hand in hers, fiercely, as though she couldn't believe I was real.

'They said they would kill you, Kate. He said if I didn't go with him, his gang would kill you and kill my family – Ammi and Asma and the baby.'

'Hush,' I said, stroking her hair. 'You're safe now, babe. You're not going anywhere, no one is going to be killed and you're not going to marry anyone.'

At least, not for a long time, I thought.

The policeman went up to her. 'We know all about the gang, Halima. We've been watching them for some time but we couldn't prove anything. The guy who abducted you was the leader and now, with your help – and with Kate's – we can charge them.'

'They had my passport,' muttered Halima. 'My real passport. In the end they said it was too dangerous to use it and they gave me a false one, but they've kept mine.'

I said nothing, but I knew what this meant.Halima's father must have given it to them. He must have gone along with this whole horrible business. Just to save his family's honour. How disgusting was that?

It was a long time before we were free to go. The police told Imran and Mahmood what was happening. I had to sign a statement and so did Halima. By the time we emerged out into the main part of the airport, dawn was breaking and the sky outside was streaked with red. The police wanted to take Halima back to college, but I told them that we had transport.

Halima emerged briefly from her daze. 'How will I get back? Whose car?'

I held her arm firmly. 'Imran's here,' I said.

She smiled up at me. 'The only family I have left,' she said. 'How did you...?'

I didn't answer. I could see Imran and Mahmood in the distance. They spotted us and Imran came running. Mahmood walked more slowly behind him, unsure of his welcome.

Imran rushed up to Halima and flung his arms round her. 'Little sister!'

She clung to him and I watched them together, the family outcasts.

She hadn't seen Mahmood yet. He stopped a little way off. Then, at last, she broke free from Imran – and looked up and saw him.

Every doubt vanished when I saw how they looked at each other.

She said nothing as he approached, but her eyes

never left his face.

He took her hand in his and kissed it, and then let it go.

CHAPTER TWENTY-FOUR

Halima

It is nearly two years since I left home. I finish college this summer.

So much has happened. I still have nightmares, but I try not to dwell on them. I try to keep positive. The gang have been prosecuted and sent to prison; none of them were here legally, so they will all be deported. But I shall never feel entirely safe. And I shall never be able to go back to my village in Pakistan.

My case has shaken the Pakistanis in Walthamstow. Opinions are still divided as to whether I did the right thing but, among people I respect, there is some sympathy for me.

And my family? They are divided too.

My father – I no longer think of him as Baba – my father went along with my abduction. He was right about one thing, the guy who took me was a cousin – but then, who isn't, in our tribe? He was a very distant cousin whom my father had promised to help with his visa and whom he had invited to Asma's wedding. I remember seeing him there and noticing his deformed finger.

Kate keeps telling me to have faith in the British legal system. I try. My father always denied having anything to do with setting up my abduction – he said he didn't hand over my passport, that I had it all the time. But everyone in the family knows that's a lie. The courts didn't believe him either, and he was prosecuted and spent several months in prison for helping the kidnappers. Sent to prison! What humiliation. He will never forgive me for that.

I have not seen my father since the day I left home. And I have no wish to see him ever again.

I speak to Asma from time to time but it's not easy. She hates what I've done to the family. As if it was my fault! I go and see her sometimes. Habib always welcomes me and it's wonderful to see my little nephew and my new baby niece, but Asma is awkward with me. We are not as we were.

And my poor Ammi, whom I love so much? She is miserable with these family splits, and she had to endure so much shame when my father went to prison – but she has not deserted me. We meet up sometimes, Ammi and I, but secretly. I never meet her at home and my father has no idea that she sees me. He has forbidden her to contact me, and this is the first time in her life that she has defied him. Her one solitary act of defiance in a life of obedience – done out of love for me.

As for Khalil – we were never close and my refusal to be forced into marriage has made him bitter towards me, stuck, as he is, in a loveless relationship.

Kate, Imran and Mahmood are my family now. Mahmood has been so brave to see me through all this. He has made trouble for himself with his own family, though he makes light of it. He tells me to be strong. All the time he tells me to be strong and have faith in the rule of law, the law of this country.

Kate tells me this, too. But she would, wouldn't she? When she leaves Oxford she wants to be a barrister and I pity anyone who gets cross-questioned by her!

Mahmood says to me that one day forced marriage will be a thing of the past, at least here in England. I hope very much that he is right. But that will probably be many years in the future. I think it will take another generation to stamp it out.

So I am trying to be strong. I'm no longer the timid girl who came to England from her village in Pakistan. I'm confident and much more worldly than I was. I've become tougher.

From now on I'm taking charge of my own life. All that time spent at Miss Brunner's debating club has stood me in good stead and I want to put my skills to use. I am determined to go into politics so that

I can make a difference – a difference to other girls like me who don't know where to turn when their family dictates their future for them.

I was lucky. I had Kate and Miss Brunner to help me. Without them, I know I wouldn't have had the courage to do what I did. And I am still lucky. I have friends who look out for me, and I have a brother – and a mother – who love me.

And I have Mahmood. Mahmood, who would give his own life for me, as I would for him.

He is beside me now as I write the final sentences of my story. And spread out on my bed is my *dupatta.* I finished it late last night. Now the final motif of the pattern is embroidered and all the sequins, beads, crystals, *kamdani* and *dabka* are in place.

Mahmood picks it up. 'Have you finished?' he asks.

I smile at him. 'My story, or my veil?' I say.

'Both.'

'Well, I've finished the *dupatta* at last,' I say. 'And for now, I suppose I've finished my story.'

He pulls me to my feet. 'Let's go, then,' he says, and we run down the familiar stairs, across the hall and out of the door. Then, hand in hand, we walk into the sunshine. Not the harsh, bleaching sun of Pakistan, but the warm, soft sunshine of a perfect English spring day.

ROSEMARY HAYES

lives and works in Cambridgeshire. She has written numerous books for children including historical and contemporary fiction and fantasy – many of which have been shortlisted for awards. She is also a reader for a well known authors' advisory service and enjoys helping unpublished writers to hone their skills.

The story of *Payback* is based on the real-life experiences of a young Muslim woman who was brave enough to defy her family and reject the husband chosen for her. She told Rosemary her story.